THE PUNISHERS

A Ripple In Time Book 3

By

VICTOR ZUGG

The Punishers

© 2020 by Victor Zugg
All rights reserved.

This is a work of **fiction**. Names, characters, businesses, places, events, and incidents are either the products of the author's imagination or used in a fictitious manner. Any resemblance to actual persons, living or dead, or actual events is purely coincidental.

VictorZuggAuthor@gmail.com

ACKNOWLEDGEMENTS

Many thanks to Brandi Doane McCann (www.ebook-coverdesigns.com) for the cover design. Once again, her creation belongs in a gallery. And equal thanks to Tamra Crow (tcrowedits@yahoo.com) for the professional editing. I'd also like to thank Cindy Vallar of Thistles & Pirates, a repository of all things pirates. The details she provided helped bring the story to life. And, of course, many thanks to Sarah Gralnick. She's always the first to read my work; I very much appreciate her suggestions. Each of these people helped make this book infinitely better.

CHAPTER 1

Two boards placed laterally across the open grave held the plain wood casket above ground.

Stephen Mason stood with his head bowed and his hands clasped in front, as did nearly everyone in the multitude of people around him, almost the entire population of Charlestown. Everyone remained motionless and quiet. A light breeze through the trees and the chirp of a blue jay in the distance were the only sounds on the chilly January day. All were dressed in their best clothes: long coats, breeches, and stockings for the men, layers of petticoats for the women. The condition of their clothes reflected their relative station in life. The crowd included all levels, from rich to poor. But no matter each person's position, everyone was equal in their reverence to the man they came to honor. Love him or hate him, none could deny William Rhett's contributions to the town. His many accomplishments would be known throughout history.

Mason had grown very close to the colonel and his family since arriving in the Charlestown area only two and a half years earlier. Without his help and friendship, Mason's life would likely be playing out much differently.

He lifted his field of view a degree or two, caught sight of Sarah, Colonel Rhett's lovely widow, and their children—William, Sarah, Catherine, and Mary—before quickly averting his gaze back to the patch of sand on which he stood. There had been three additional children the colonel had spoken of, but they had died early in life. In addition to Sarah Rhett and the children, the former Mary Trott, now William Jr.'s wife, stood next to him as a member of the family. And next to her stood Nicholas and Jane Trott, her father and mother. Nicholas was the former chief justice of South Carolina and Colonel Rhett's closest friend. The seven of them stood in a tight group at the head of the casket. Their expressions remained stoic, despite the loss. There was not a single tear in the bunch. That was the way for people of this time. Death was a common occurrence. It was best to pay respect, say goodbye, and move on with life.

It was three hundred years in the future when Mason last stood in this exact spot. An inscribed stone vault flashed through his mind. In the coming weeks, Colonel Rhett's casket would be exhumed and placed inside that vault. The date of his birth and death would be carved on the lid—*September 4th, 1666 – January 12, 1722*. In reality, the year he died, the current year, was 1723, under the Gregorian calendar. But the colonies at this time still used the Julian calendar. The new year under that calendar wouldn't start until March 25th. For the current era, 1723 hadn't started yet.

Where Mason now stood, in the middle of Church Street in front of St. Philip's Episcopal Church, would one day be paved over but would continue to divide the church from its cemetery. Through eternity William Rhett would have a front row seat to the church's main entrance.

Mason twisted his body as he glanced at the rough-brick structure behind him, with its three porticos and the tall, cupola-topped bell tower. Its construction would soon be completed, and its members would celebrate their first Easter in the new church. The brick church would serve the community for a hundred years before succumbing to a fire. Mason knew these things because he had read them in a history book. In a hundred years a new church, with the same layout, only a little larger, would be built on the same spot. It was that new church that Mason had toured during his return to the future two years earlier. The future—the 21st century. That was his rightful time. At least it was. This was his life now. Three hundred years in the past from his former life as a federal air marshal. A lot had happened since being hurled through those years by a freak storm over the Atlantic, with a plane load of accidental time travelers.

He glanced to his right at his wife, the former Karen James, one of the attendants on that ill-fated flight. She held the tiny hand of their almost two-year-old son, Michael, who was growing impatient and beginning to fidget. To Mason's left stood Jeremy and Lisa Jackson, the only other remaining survivors from that flight. The four of them, now five, were carving a living from a rice plantation. Their success had been in large part due to the man lying in the casket before them.

A man clearing his throat brought Mason from his reverie.

Mason raised his head and turned his attention to that man. He was young, mid-thirties, and he stood tall and straight.

Reverend Alexander Gardner's thoughtful eyes scanned the gathering before clearing his throat again. "I didn't know William very well, but I do know he contributed much to this community."

The reverend cited Rhett's many deeds. He spoke with passion and compassion, as men of God often do. But in truth, Mason was well aware that William Rhett, of late, had found himself on the wrong side of the community's conventional wisdom. In 1719, during the bloodless coup when nearly everyone opted for crown rule over the Carolina Colony, Rhett sided with the former colony proprietors, a private consortium of aristocratic English owners. Rhett and Trott, preferring independent governance, were the two loudest voices against the crown. That position put them on the outs with the vast majority of residents.

Mason scanned the somber faces in the crowd. All of Rhett's major detractors were in attendance, for even they recognized Charlestown may well have not survived had it not been for the man in the coffin.

When Reverend Gardner stopped talking, several men circled the grave and positioned ropes under both ends of the casket. They pulled the ropes taut and lifted the casket, while other men removed the boards. The casket was then slowly lowered into the ground.

The reverend gave a slight nod at Sarah.

She stepped forward, took a handful of earth from the nearby mound, and let the grains sift through her fingers and fall onto the casket. Each member of the family did the same, followed by the Trotts, and then others from the crowd wishing to show their respect.

Mason and his cadre joined the queue. Each paused for a moment to say a silent prayer after depositing a handful of dirt. When Mason and Karen had paid their respects a final time, they made their way over to Sarah Rhett and the children.

"He will be missed," Mason said.

Sarah looked around at the crowd beginning to disperse. "By some."

"We appreciate everyone who came out," William Jr. said.

"If there's anything we can do," Karen said, "please don't hesitate to ask. We'd be happy to help."

Sarah tightened her arm wrapped around William Jr.'s waist. "William here has been handling the day-to-day for some time."

William Rhett's manner of death was a matter of history—a stroke is what Mason had read of the account, so he elected to forego the questions many others had already asked. "Charlie and I will stop by in a few days to see how you're doing."

Sarah looked around the thinning crowd. "Where is that Charlie Sievert?"

Mason spotted him with a shovel in his hand, pitching dirt into the grave along with three other men.

"He hasn't said much," Sarah said.

"It was quite a shock for all of us, but especially for Charlie," Karen said. "He's dealing with it in his own way."

"He would be the first to step up if you needed anything," Mason said.

"I know," Sarah said. "Charlie can be a rascal, but he's a good man."

Mason stared at Charlie. This was one of the few times Mason had seen him completely sober. He turned back to Sarah. "When will the vault be finished?"

"Two or three weeks," she said. "They're engraving the lid."

"If I can, I'd like to be here when the colonel is laid to his final rest," Mason said. He looked around as Jeremy and Lisa approached. "We all would."

"Of course," Sarah said with a slight smile.

Mason shook hands with William Jr. and Mr. Trott, winked at the children, and then put his arm around Karen's shoulders. "See you in a few days," he said, as he turned and stepped off.

When they were a few feet away, Karen leaned her head closer to Mason. "Will they be okay?"

Mason glanced back at the Rhett family. "Do you really want to know?"

"I do," Sarah said.

"Jane Trott dies in five years and Judge Trott marries the widow Rhett almost immediately. He moves into the Rhett house."

"Oh. That's probably more than I really needed to know."

"Should we pitch in and help Charlie?" Jeremy asked, as he and Lisa caught up.

Mason turned and peered at Charlie, still shoveling dirt into the grave along with the three other men. "Let him handle it," he said, as he turned and continued walking.

They stopped under the church's portico and watched the procession of people leaving the cemetery.

"When are you making the run to New York?" Karen asked.

"We would already be there, if not for Colonel Rhett's untimely death." He looked to the sky. "Weather looks stable enough. Might as well head out early tomorrow." He glanced at Jeremy. "Me and Jeremy. Charlie will remain behind, as usual."

"I still can't get over how sudden this happened," Lisa said. "He's fine one day, and dead the next."

"History identified it as a stroke," Mason said. "It probably was. I know he was under a lot of stress lately, with the trial and all."

"That was all truly ridiculous," Karen said. "Grown men accusing each other of smuggling."

"It probably wouldn't have gone anywhere, except that the colonel was accusing the crown's governor," Jeremy said.

Mason twisted his lips. "It was deeper than that. Governor Nicholson detested Colonel Rhett, and the colonel felt the same way about him."

"The colonel might have won the law suit if he'd bothered to show up," Karen said. "At the very least he could have argued for a mitigated finding."

"Yeah, that four hundred pound fine really pissed him off," Jeremy said. "That's probably what caused the stroke."

"Sarah hasn't said much about his last days," Mason said. "And I'm not going to ask."

Lisa pulled the shawl around her shoulders tighter. "How much longer are we going to stand here?"

Mason glanced at Charlie, walking in their direction. "We should be good to go."

◆◆◆

"It never ceases to amaze me," Mason said, as he stared at the Manhattan coastline in the distance.

"What?" Jeremy asked.

"The city's very humble beginnings, versus what it will become in the future."

"It won't smell as bad," Jeremy said.

"True." Mason scanned the sloop's deck, ensuring all was ready for docking at their normal perch along the wharves. He glanced at the mainsail and the jib, both stretched tight with the wind, and then judged the distance to his particular dock. He looked back at Jeremy manning the tiller. This would be only their third trip to New York and Mason had docked the boat the two previous times. He had no doubt Jeremy could do as well, without any directions. Without comment, Mason stepped to the mast, glanced at the approaching wharves, and began lowering the sail. Twenty minutes later, barely moving, with only a few feet between the boat and the dock, he tossed a line to a man hurrying over to help. Mason thanked the man as he lashed the bow and stern lines to the dock's wood cleats.

With only a slight nod, the man walked away.

"I'll check in with Pappy," Mason said, as he leapt to the dock.

Jeremy immediately began untying a two-wheeled, two-handled cart, about the size of a wheelbarrow, lashed to the deck just behind the mast.

Mason returned a few minutes later and helped Jeremy transfer the cart to the dock.

"We should have thought of this last year," Jeremy said.

"True enough," Mason agreed, as he slung open the hatch to the small storage cabin below deck, in the bow. "And the year before."

He and Jeremy began transferring the six bags of Spanish silver coins to the cart.

"What do you think, two more of these trips to get Misses Stewart paid?"

"Two more seasons like this one should do it," Mason said.

"You plan to continue making the trips to St. Augustine?"

"I think so," Mason said. "Trade for the silver as long as we can."

With the bags of silver loaded on the cart, Jeremy returned to the sloop and retrieved a canvas satchel containing a flintlock pistol, a box of paper cartridges, and his log book. With the satchel in hand, he leapt back to the dock. "Ready to roll."

With his left elbow, Mason patted the shoulder holster under his coat as the two of them started off. The holster contained his Glock 9mm and two extra magazines.

They followed the usual route through town, until they stood in front of Misses Stewart's house on Gold Street. Just like the two previous years, Mason knocked on the door and was greeted by Ernest, the butler.

Ernest motioned for the two men to enter.

Mason and Jeremy ferried the six bags of silver and the satchel to just inside the door.

Ernest closed the door, led the two men into the parlor, and motioned toward a couple of straight back chairs. "I'll fetch Misses Wilma, if you would care to wait here," he said with his perpetual neutral expression.

When Ernest left the room, Mason stepped back to the foyer, retrieved a single bag of silver and Jeremy's satchel, and returned to his chair in the parlor. He placed the items on the floor at his feet.

They had been waiting nearly ten minutes when Ernest returned with a silver tea service, which he sat on the salon table in the middle of the room. "The Misses will be with you shortly."

At just that moment, Misses Stewart rushed into the room struggling with a length of hair that wouldn't stay in place. "I am sorry. I was out back."

Mason and Jeremy stood, and remained standing until she motioned to their chairs. "Please, take your seats, gentlemen," she said, as she took her usual spot on the mostly white settee. She smoothed her several layers of petticoats with the palm of her hand as she settled in. "You're a bit early this year."

"Yes, ma'am," Mason said. "We didn't think you would mind."

"Of course not," she said with a smile. "I look forward to your visits. And it's not just because of the payments. I like to hear the news back in Charlestown. So, tell me, what is happening back home?" She motioned for Ernest to pour the tea.

He did so and handed a cup each to Mason and Jeremy.

Mason took a sip, rested the cup and saucer on his knee, and assumed a more somber expression. "Unfortunately, the colonel has died."

Misses Stewart cocked her head to one side. "I didn't think that old codger would ever die, too mean. What happened?"

Mason went into great detail about the political climate in Charlestown and how Colonel Rhett and Nicholas Trott ended up on the short end. He explained the slander suits, Rhett's loss to the governor, and his subsequent death from what appeared to be apoplexy.

They talked on for a full hour before Mason and Jeremy ran out of news and the conversation began to wane. They concluded their business with the silver and said their goodbyes.

Back on the street, Jeremy pulled the now much lighter cart as the two of them made their way back toward the wharves.

"Let's pop into Gerber's Tavern and see what Forrest has cooked up for dinner," Mason said.

They made a slight detour, parked the cart in front of the tavern on Wall Street, and entered.

Mason spotted Forrest behind the bar, leaning against the wood structure with both arms outstretched. His head hung between his biceps as though he were dog-tired. Mason scanned the interior. It was absent any patrons, except for three men sitting at a corner table, each with a mug before them. They talked quietly among themselves.

Forrest looked up at Mason and Jeremy as they approached the bar. He attempted a smile but it failed to reflect his normal jovial self.

"You don't look so good, my friend," Mason said. "Are you feeling alright?"

"Dog-tired, Mason. My legs feel like wet noodles."

"Your face is flushed," Jeremy said.

Mason leaned over the bar and put his back hand against Forrest's forehead. "Feels damp and a little warm." He cocked his head and peered at Forrest's neck. "That blotch looks like some kind of rash." Mason stepped back, removed his three-cornered hat, and ran his fingers through his hair. He turned to Jeremy. "Until we know what's what, why don't you wait outside."

Jeremy stared at him with a confused look.

"Trust me on this."

"What about you?"

"I'll be fine. Just wait outside. I'll be with you shortly."

Jeremy twisted his lips, stared at Mason a few seconds, turned, and walked out.

Mason turned back to Forrest. "How long you been feeling this way?"

Forrest thought a few moments and finally shook his head. "I don't know, couple of days, maybe. Been sweating like crazy and I've had a headache at least that long."

Mason took in a deep breath and exhaled. He pursed his lips as he stared into the man's eyes.

"I think I'm sick," Forrest said.

"I think you're right."

CHAPTER 2

"Anyone else sick around here?"

"Business has been down the last few days," Forrest said. "Maybe." He rubbed his face with one hand. He closed his eyes as he turned his head toward the tobacco stained ceiling. "You remember I mentioned my friend, Bill." He looked back down at Mason. "We took over this place together."

"I do," Mason said. "He died a few years back."

"Pretty sure it was typhoid," Forrest said. "And his symptoms were the same as what I have now. And the previous owner died of the same thing." He peered long and hard at Mason. "I think my ticket may be up."

Interesting choice of words, Mason thought. "I would have to agree," Mason said.

Forrest gave a slight nod and let his chin sink to his chest.

"About the first part. The symptoms seem to be classic. But I have something that may help with the second part."

Forrest angled his eyes up to Mason and slowly raised his head. "What?"

"Unfortunately, it's back in Charlestown. We're three days away. Can you hold on that long?"

"I can try," Forrest said. "But what is it?"

"Think of it as an herbal medicine. It will work if we can get you to it quickly. We'd need to leave right now. Is there someone who can look after the store?"

Forrest reached into his coat pocket and produced a key. "Tom," he yelled across the room.

All three men at the table turned to Forrest.

Forrest tossed the key to them.

One of the men caught it in midair. He peered at the metal object in the palm of his hand and then looked up at Forrest.

"Take care of the place," Forrest said. "I'll be gone a few days, maybe a little longer."

"Sure, Forrest," the man said, apparently Tom. He returned to his conversation with the two men at the table.

"I'm ready when you are," Forrest said to Mason.

"You have a bath tub in this joint?"

"I do," Forrest said.

"I need you to take a bath. Use lots of soap everywhere, especially your hair."

"What for?"

"If it's typhoid, it can be passed by lice. Burn the clothes you have on, and then put on something clean."

"It will have to be a cold bath," Forrest said.

"Good, that will help lower any fever you have. Do you need help?"

"I can manage," Forrest said, as he started shuffling toward the back room. "I'll meet you outside."

Mason exited the tavern.

"What's the story?" Jeremy asked.

Mason winced. "I think he may have typhoid."

"Is that contagious?"

"It is or, at least, it can be. It's usually a result of bad sanitation." He looked around at the streets. "Like they have around here. His business partner probably died from it, and maybe the previous owner. Typhoid, yellow fever, and malaria are rampant, but mostly during the summer. Except typhoid. Badly managed sanitation gets into the water and food."

"So, what's he going to do? Is there a treatment in this time?"

"For him there is," Mason said. "The antibiotics I brought back from my excursion into the future."

"You have some with you?"

"No, it's back at the plantation. Which is why we're taking him back with us."

Jeremy raised both eyebrows and stared at Mason. "You said it was contagious."

"Karen and I have been vaccinated because of our previous jobs. You, Lisa, and everyone else will keep your distance. Body lice can result in human to human transfer of the germ. Forrest is taking a bath and will burn the clothes he had on. That should help."

"But even if Lisa and I come down with it—"

"The antibiotics. I brought back plenty of Cipro and it has a long shelf life."

Jeremy's body visibly relaxed. The stress lines on his face faded.

"Why don't you take the cart back to the boat and get us ready to head out. Forrest and I will be along shortly."

"Do we have enough food and water for the three of us?"

"Forrest won't have much of an appetite. And we have plenty of water."

"I'll see you at the boat," Jeremy said, as he turned, took hold of the cart, and started off.

Forrest emerged from the tavern thirty minutes later, looking more refreshed but still weak. He held a cloth satchel in one hand. "Ready."

They began walking toward the wharves.

◆◆◆

The bundle of blankets on the aft deck stirred and Jeremy's head emerged from the folds. "How long was I out?" he asked, staring up at Mason.

Mason stood with his hand on the tiller. "About four hours," he said, without taking his eyes off the fading horizon. "It will be dark soon."

"How's Forrest?" Jeremy asked, as he got to his feet.

"Take the tiller and I'll go check on him."

Jeremy took hold of the handle. "While you're down there, I could use something to eat."

"Will do," Mason said, as he began making his way along the rolling deck. He opened the forward hatch and peered into the darkness before climbing down. He found Forrest where he had left him, rolled in a blanket and a couple of layers of sail cloth. Only his head was visible. His body undulated back and forth with the boat's movement.

Mason put the back of his hand to Forrest's forehead. *Warm.* And even in the subdued light it was evident Forrest was quivering.

Forrest turned his head and opened his eyes. "Bill?" he mumbled.

"Mason. How are you feeling?"

An expression of recognition spread over Forrest's face. "About how I probably look."

"Yeah, you've seen better days, and you will again."

"How much longer?"

"We're still a day out. If the wind holds, I'm hoping to arrive before dark tomorrow afternoon." He reached for a canteen and removed the cork. "You need to keep drinking water."

"Isn't that what made me sick?"

"Probably, but this water has been boiled. It's safe." With one hand, he helped Forrest raise his head as he brought the canteen to his lips.

Forrest took two sips and then turned his head slightly signaling he'd had enough. "Rum would taste better."

"No doubt, but you'd end up even more dehydrated than you already are," Mason said. He put the canteen back to his lips. "Two more sips."

Forrest did as he was told.

Mason returned the cork, sat the canteen within Forrest's easy reach, and then sat with his back against the hull. "Can you eat something?"

"I don't think so. Not sure if it's the typhoid or this boat."

"Maybe a little of both. Have you slept at all?"

"Not much. Just dozing. This boat, my shivering, and the freezing cold make it hard to sleep." He pulled the blanket tighter around his neck.

"There's not much I can do about that," Mason said. "You'll have to tough it out."

"I can do that. I've done it before."

Mason thought a few moments as he stared down at Forrest. "When we first met, you said something about being in the Navy."

"I said I spent time with the Navy."

Mason cocked his head.

"It's a long story," Forrest said. "Better for another time."

Mason nodded as he began getting to his feet. "Try to sleep some. I'll check on you in a couple of hours."

"Thanks, Mason. I really appreciate what you are trying to do here."

"Not a problem, my friend. You would do the same thing."

"I'd like to think so," he responded.

"I'll be back in a while," Mason said, as he climbed the ladder. He exited the opening, closed the hatch, and rejoined Jeremy at the helm.

"How's he doing?"

"Fever. The rash on his neck is worse. No appetite and nausea may be setting in."

"And?"

"As long as he's conscious enough to swallow those pills, he'll pull through."

Mason checked on Forrest several times during the night. In the early morning he managed to get about four hours of sleep. He rose from his bundle of blankets on deck to find Jeremy still on duty at the tiller. "Everything okay?" he grumbled.

"Wind is steady. Some clouds on the horizon, but I think we'll miss them."

"Let me check on Forrest and then I'll spell you," Mason said, as he got to his feet. As soon as he opened the forward hatch, he could hear Forrest uttering mostly incoherent words mixed with varying degrees of moans, like a bad dream. Mason climbed down the ladder and knelt next to Forrest's uncovered body. He had obviously thrown the blankets and sail cloth to the side during the preceding four hours. He tossed and turned. Despite the coolness of the air, sweat beaded on his face.

"We're going in," Forrest suddenly yelled. "Brace!" He then went into an incoherent moan.

Mason put his hand on Forrest's shoulder and shook him gently. He called out his name.

Forrest continued to moan. "Ditching," he screamed.

Mason shook the man's shoulder more forcibly. "Forrest, wake up." He positioned the blankets and sail cloth back around his body in a makeshift sleeping bag.

Forrest stopped moaning and began to settle. After a few moments his eyes flittered and then opened. He stared up at Mason without recognition.

"It's Mason, you're still on the sloop."

"Mason," he groaned.

"How do you feel?"

"The worst I've ever felt," Forrest said, as he shivered.

"Hang in there, we only have a few more hours," Mason said, as he opened the canteen and helped Forrest take a couple of gulps. "Can you eat anything?"

"Any bread?"

"Sorry, just salt pork and some cheese."

"Don't think I could hold that down."

Mason nodded as he sat back. "Tell me Forrest, where did you say you were from?"

"I didn't," Forrest said. He stared at Mason several moments. "Did I say something in my sleep?"

"Some."

"Anything intelligible?"

"Not really," Mason said. "So, where were you before you arrived here on the east coast?"

Forrest stared at Mason for several moments. "I was in—"

Mason peered at Forrest with anticipation.

"Look," Forrest said, "it's complicated."

"I'm pretty good at understanding complicated." Mason paused to steady his balance as the boat hit a wave. "Go ahead, you were about to tell me where you came from."

"Fort Lauderdale." Forrest stared at Mason, expecting a confused look to appear. It didn't.

Mason nodded. "Pilot?"

A shocked expression slowly spread over Forrest's face. He blinked one time, long and slow.

"What year?" Mason asked.

"Wait, you know about Fort Lauderdale?"

"Tip of Florida. Near Miami. I know it well. At least I will in about three hundred years."

"Three hundred years?"

"Jeremy and I, along with a plane load of passengers, arrived here from the year 2020."

Forrest wiped beads of sweat from his forehead as he reclined his head down on a makeshift pillow of rolled up sailcloth. "I get it. I'm dreaming." He closed his eyes.

"You're not dreaming."

Forrest opened his eyes and turned his head toward Mason.

"I had a feeling you were different. Your manner of speech and word usage."

"You, too," Forrest said. "The year 2020 you say?"

"Yep. And you?"

"The year of our Lord nineteen hundred and forty-five. US Marine, flying a Navy Avenger."

Mason narrowed his eyebrows. "Flight 19?"

"Yeah," Forrest said. "But how—"

"The loss of those five Avengers is, or will be, a matter of history and remained a mystery in my time, seventy-five years after the fact." He stared at Forrest for several moments. "So, finally the mystery is solved. What happened?"

"Flew into a storm and poof, we were here. At least Bill Lightfoot and I ended up here after ditching in the Atlantic. We were separated from the other four planes." He turned away and shook his head. "I don't know what happened to the other guys." He looked up at Mason. "How many of you made it?"

"Thirty-two made it to shore. There are only four of us now."

"Thirty-two?" Forrest asked. "How many did you start with?"

"Over a hundred."

"On one plane?"

"Airliner. Think of a very large DC-3 or C-47 with jet engines. Complete with meals and drinks. Thousands of them will fly constantly. Some will carry over three hundred people."

Forrest snorted. "Airliners."

Mason nodded.

"So, thirty-two people from the future walked into Charlestown?"

"No. We acquired a sloop, similar to this one, and were headed in that direction when we ran into a pirate. That pirate killed nearly everyone on the sloop."

"And only four of you made it."

"Basically," Mason said. "Actually, five."

Forrest stared at the overhead for several moments. "With the aid of a passing fishing boat, and after a great deal of confusion, Bill and I made our way to New York and eventually found work in the tavern. We wanted to remain as visible as possible, hoping others in our group had survived and would make their way to town."

"When did you come to understand you were in a different time?"

"Well, the people on the fishing boat seemed very odd. They spoke English, but none of them understood what we were telling them, about ditching and all. But it wasn't until we arrived in New York that we finally came to accept the obvious. We walked around in a state of confusion for a couple of days."

"How did you end up owning the tavern?"

"The owner got sick. And with no living relatives, he verbally willed the place to Bill and I on his death bed. The gift was witnessed by several people. That was over ten years ago."

"And none of the other crew members ever showed up?"

"Not a one." He wiped his forehead with his sleeve. "I guess it's lucky you came along. What're these herbs you have for me?"

"Antibiotics."

"Penicillin?"

"Something much better. A lot changed, mostly for the better, over the seventy-five years between our two times."

Forrest rested his head back against the mound of sailcloth. He took in a deep breath and exhaled. He suddenly shot Mason a piercing look. "So, you know how we ended up here?"

"Not really. Flew into a storm, just like you, and poof. But with one difference. I've made the trip three times."

CHAPTER 3

Forrest raised both eyebrows. "You know how to get back?"

"Not really," Mason said. "It was happenstance all three times, two times while flying through a storm, and once on the ocean's surface. But I was pretty out of it that time. I don't remember what happened."

"But you made it back."

"Yeah," Mason said, as he ran his hand over his thick beard. "For my third trip, my return to this time, I was in search of that storm. And I found it. But I was flying at twenty-five thousand feet."

"You returned to the future and then purposefully came back. Why would you do that?"

"Long story," Mason said, as he leaned in and peered at Forrest's face. "How you feeling?"

"Terrible. Wet noodle. I'm not sure I can even walk."

Mason helped him drink from the canteen. "Get some rest. I need to spell Jeremy, but we can talk more later."

Forrest gave a slight nod.

"I'll check on you in a while," Mason said, as he pulled the quilt closer to Forrest's neck, before raising to a stooped position in the cramped quarters. He glanced at Forrest a final time as he climbed the ladder. He joined Jeremy at the helm. "Forrest is a fellow time traveler," he said nonchalantly.

Jeremy jerked his head around to Mason. "What?"

"Yeah, he was a member of a 1945 Navy training flight out of Fort Lauderdale. Five planes that never returned. Torpedo bombers. It remained a mystery for over seventy-five years. Now we know."

"Five planes? How many people?"

"Fourteen or fifteen, I think. Forrest got separated from the others in a storm, ended up ditching. He and Bill, his fellow crew member, made it to New York. You know the rest."

Jeremy peered at Mason several moments before he finally spoke. "That's unbelievable."

"Really?" Mason asked. "How could it be that unbelievable when you and I went through the same thing?"

"You have a point." Jeremy thought for a moment. "I wonder how many others from the future are scattered around these parts?"

"Stands to reason there would be more," Mason said, as he took the tiller from Jeremy. "You may want to get some rest. We can all talk to him more about it when we get back to the plantation."

"How's he feeling?"

"Worse," Mason said with a look of concern.

Jeremy scanned the thin white shoreline in the distance and then looked up at the billowing mainsail. "Let's hope the wind holds." Without further comment, he slid into his makeshift bed on deck, threw a blanket over his body, and rolled to his side with his face only inches from the hull.

◆◆◆

"Go let Karen and Lisa know what's going on," Mason said, as he stepped onto the dock with a bow line in hand. "You and Lisa keep your distance while I get Forrest up and moving. We'll put him in the extra bedroom. And keep Michael away."

Jeremy jumped to the dock and hurried off.

Mason stepped back aboard the boat, opened the forward hatch, and dropped down through the opening.

Forrest was on his back, with his eyes closed. His breathing was shallow.

Mason rousted him by the shoulder until his eyes finally opened. "We're here," he said, as he began lifting Forrest's torso. "Can you stand?"

"I can try," Forrest mumbled.

Mason got him to a sitting position and helped him roll to his knees.

On all fours, Forrest crawled to the ladder and slowly began making his way up, with Mason's help.

With both of them on deck, Mason got Forrest to his feet.

Despite his wobbly legs, Forrest raised up to his full height for the first time in three days. He stood nearly as tall as Mason's six feet, but with a slenderer physique. His clothes were rumpled and his near shoulder-length, black hair was in disarray. He scanned the plantation house and the fields beyond. His eyes locked on something. "Is that Karen or Lisa walking this way?"

Mason looked up. "That's Karen. She and I have been inoculated against Typhoid. You'll be moving into a guest room in the house." He also saw young Michael scamper down the back-porch stairs and begin waddling his way toward the dock, all the while babbling his incoherent baby talk.

Lisa scooped him up before he had gone very far and returned him to the porch. With her perpetual trim figure and signature blond hair, she stood with Michael in her arms, watching the activities unfold.

Jeremy came out of the house and stood beside them.

"Does she know about me?" Forrest asked.

"She knows you exist," Mason said. He tightened his lips as Karen came within talking distance.

"You must be Forrest," Karen said with a smile, as she approached the boat. She stepped aboard and dipped under Forrest's other arm to help support him.

They helped Forrest, on unsteady legs, over the gunwale and onto the dock. The three of them made their way slowly across the ground.

"You need hep, Mista Mason?" Sylvester asked, as he approached, but still in the distance.

"It's alright, Sylvester. This is Forrest Gerber, a good friend. He's come down with the fever and will be staying with us for a while. Everyone except Karen and I will need to keep their distance until his fever breaks. Please let Charlie know when you see him."

Sylvester, still thirty yards away, stopped walking. "Yes, sir, Mista Mason. I'll let 'em know." He turned and started walking toward the work barn.

"Where is Charlie?" Mason asked Karen.

"His room in the work barn, I guess. We probably won't see him until tomorrow morning."

"Does he drink more, or less, when I'm gone?"

"About the same."

"Who's Charlie?" Forrest mumbled.

"He manages the plantation," Mason said. "Good man, hard working. Most of all, he can be trusted."

"So, he knows about your past?"

"No, not that," Mason said. "I'm not sure anyone from this era would be able to understand."

"We don't even understand it," Karen said. "Jeremy briefly mentioned your situation."

Jeremy opened the back door to the house and then stepped to the side.

Mason and Karen practically carried Forrest up the stairs and directly to the guest bedroom at the end of the hall.

Lisa and Jeremy stood in the hall and watched from the open door as Mason lowered Forrest to the bed. "I'll need my med kit and some water," he said, glancing at Lisa.

Lisa disappeared down the hall.

Mason and Karen removed Forrest's boots and clothes.

Karen immediately gathered the bundle into her arms and left the room.

Jeremy looked on, still from the open doorway, as Mason tucked Forrest under the covers.

Lisa returned to the doorway with the black nylon, zippered med kit and a large mug of water. She tossed the kit to Mason and placed the water on the floor just inside the threshold.

Mason unzipped the kit and took out a large, amber-colored glass bottle full of white pills. He unscrewed the plastic cap from the bottle and dumped two pills into the palm of his hand. "We'll start with a loading dose," he said to Forrest. He retrieved the mug of water, returned to Forrest's bedside, and lifted his head. "I need you to swallow these," he said, as he brought his palm up to Forrest's mouth.

Forrest, having trouble focusing his eyes, opened his mouth.

Mason dumped the two pills into his mouth and then lifted the mug to his lips. "Take some water and swallow those pills," he commanded.

Karen returned to the room and knelt on the opposite side of the bed. "How much you giving him?"

"That was two, two hundred and fifty milligram tablets. Let's do another five hundred milligrams in twelve hours. Then we'll drop back to two-fifty every twelve hours. He should be feeling much better in a couple of days." He rose to his full height next to the bed. "Let him sleep," he said, as he sat the bottle of tablets and the mug of water on the small table next to the bed. "What did you do with his clothes?"

"In the cooking pot to boil," she said. "I put his boots outside."

Mason nodded as he motioned for Karen to follow him out of the room.

They stepped into the hallway with Lisa and Jeremy. Mason closed the door behind him.

"What do you think?" Lisa asked.

"I don't know," Mason said. "We'll have to wait and see." He looked at Karen. "One of us should probably stay with him through tonight."

Karen tightened her lips in agreement. "You and Jeremy get some rest. I'll stay with Forrest once I get a pan of water and a wash cloth."

Everyone stared at her.

"For the forehead," she said, "to cool his fever."

◆◆◆

Forrest opened his eyes and peered at the face of an angel. Blurry, but an angel nonetheless. "Am I dead?" he murmured.

"No, you're alive," Karen said. She plucked the folded wash cloth from his forehead, dipped it in the pan of water, wrung out the excess, and returned it to his head. "How are you feeling?"

Forrest blinked several times. Karen's face came into focus. "Weak. And thirsty."

"You've been asleep for sixteen hours straight, except for a minute four hours ago for your second dose of antibiotics." She lifted his head and placed a second pillow. "Feel like you can drink something?"

"I think so. Still a bit nauseous, but not as bad as before."

Karen put a mug to his lips. "Drink it all if you can."

Forrest gulped down the water and then turned his head slightly, signaling he'd had enough. The last few drops splattered against his upper lip.

Karen dabbed with a dry cloth. "Can you eat something?"

"I think so. Maybe just some bread."

Karen started up from her chair at his bedside.

"Wait," he said, as he looked around the room.

"How did I get here?" He looked under the covers at his nude body. "And who took my clothes?"

"Mason and Jeremy brought you here from New York on the sloop. You were conscious, but just barely."

"And my clothes?"

"We boiled them. They're ready when you want them."

"Am I going to live?" he asked, as he stared into Karen's eyes.

"I think so. You arrived here just in time."

"Here?"

"Charlestown."

"Your plantation?"

"That's right."

"I'm starting to remember now. Mason brought the antibiotics when he came back through time."

"Lucky for you," Karen said. "You're not as feverish as you were. I think it may be breaking."

"Where's Mason?"

"Outside, seeing to things. We took turns with you during the night."

He turned his head toward the window and the sunlight pouring through the glass panes. "Just the four of you left from an airliner. Hard to believe."

"Impossible to believe, but I understand you had a similar experience. Mason told me everything you said."

"I thought I was stuck here forever," Forrest said. "But Mason found a way back."

"By accident. I'm sure he told you."

"Yeah. Well, not the details. But there's a way."

"Maybe. If you're willing to spend the rest of your life looking for that one-in-a-million chance."

Forrest gave a slight nod. "Yeah." He glanced around the room. "Am I the first one to benefit from your antibiotics?"

"No, we had a couple of typhoid cases among the workers until we improved the sanitation. The antibiotics saved their lives. Mason also brought back some antimalarial drugs. But treating that particular parasite can be tricky. And we still have yellow fever to contend with."

"The workers?"

"Slaves, but we don't think of them that way. We've tried to make conditions here as comfortable as this time period will allow. Mason, Jeremy, Charlie, and some of the workers have rebuilt their cabins. They're bigger now and more insulated from the weather and insects. They have a common shower rigged with water barrels down by the cottages. There's two of them on the property. The other is outside our back door. We all eat in a common kitchen and dining hall. Sickness has been much reduced. We even educate those wanting to learn."

Forrest shifted to more of a sitting position. "And the locals have gone along with all that?"

"The changes have been gradual. On purpose."

Forrest nodded.

"You want something with that bread?"

"Nothing greasy. Just the bread for now."

"Be right back," Karen said. She stood and stepped off toward the door. She pointed to one corner of the room. "There's a chamber pot if you need it."

He went to throw the covers off but stopped when he remembered he was nude. "I'll try. If you hear a thump it means I didn't make it." He gave her half a smile.

"You're a marine," she smiled. "You'll manage. Be right back with that bread."

He waited until the door closed behind her, pulled the covers back, and slid one leg over the side, followed by the second leg. He came to a sitting position, pivoted, and placed both feet on the cold, pine slatted floor. He pushed himself up and kept a hand on the bed while he tested the strength of his legs. It felt like his feet were buried in concrete, but he was able to move them without falling. He made his way to the chamber pot, using various pieces of furniture to keep his balance.

He urinated in the pot more than he thought he would and then slowly made his way back to the bed.

He had just slid under the covers when the door opened.

Mason walked in with a small bowl containing a couple of chunks of bread. A smile spread across his face. "Karen said you've rejoined the living."

"Some. Whether it takes remains to be seen."

"You'll be fine," he said, as he placed the bowl on the side table, refilled the mug with water from a pitcher, then took a seat in the chair. "You'll be up in no time." He glanced around the room. "Were you able to use the chamber pot?"

"Yeah. My legs worked better than I thought."

"That's good," Mason said, as he placed the bowl of bread on the side of the bed. "Try to eat something. Let's see how you do."

Forrest brought one of the chunks to his mouth and nibbled small bits from one corner. Gradually, he increased the size of each bite.

As they talked, he ate and drank. "You haven't been sick from the water?"

"We get our water from a well. But we still strain and boil all drinking water, even for the workers. It's nearly a full-time job for one of the women."

"Look, I'm really sorry to impose on you like this."

"Are you kidding?" Mason said with a snort. "A fellow time traveler is always welcome. For as long as you want to stay."

After finishing one of the two chunks of bread, Forrest handed the bowl to Mason. "I think I'm good for now."

Mason placed the bowl on the side table and handed Forrest the mug of water. "Drink some more. We don't want your kidneys to freeze up."

Forrest took two gulps and gave the mug back to Mason. "Will there be a problem in hauling my ass back to New York?"

"No problem at all, but we were hoping you'd hang around for a while. Think of it as a vacation."

"Thanks, Mason."

The sound of two raps on the door interrupted the two men. The door opened a few inches, exposing Charlie's face and rumpled hat.

"Sorry, but we need you down at the dock," Charlie said.

Mason glanced back at Forrest. "Forrest, this is Charlie. Charlie this is Forrest. He'll be staying with us for a while. He should be on his feet in a couple of days."

"Hopefully, sooner than that," Forrest said. "Nice to meet you, Charlie."

"I better see what's up," Mason said. "Get some more rest and drink the water. Karen will be in to check on you in a while."

"Will do," Forrest said, as Mason stood.

"What's happening?" Mason asked, as he stepped into the hallway with Charlie and closed the door behind him.

"We have company," Charlie said, "and they don't appear all that friendly. Arthur Sullivan."

They started walking.

"The broker?" Mason said, as they descended the stairs and exited the back door. "The season is done, why would the rice broker be here now?"

"He just said to find you. Provost Marshal Loughton is with him, and there's four other men."

"The provost marshal," Mason said, as he peered at the group of men at the dock. He saw Jeremy heading that way from the barn.

The group stared in unison at Mason's and Charlie's approach. Serious expressions revealed nothing about the reason for their visit.

"Mister Sullivan," Mason said, as he walked up. "To what do I owe the pleasure?"

Sullivan nodded at Loughton. "You're under arrest, Mister Mason. You'll need to come with us."

CHAPTER 4

Mason stopped in his tracks just as he was about to raise his hand to shake. He stared at the rather rotund man in his expensive breeches and coat for several moments, trying to gauge whether he was joking. It didn't appear that he was. "What's the charge?"

"What's going on?" Jeremy asked as he walked up and stopped next to Mason.

"Mister Sullivan here says I'm under arrest. He was about to tell me why."

James Loughton, a man of medium height and weight, on the young side for a provost marshal, took a step forward. He wore long pants and a coat, both somewhat wrinkled. He was relatively new to the position, and had been an improvement over the previous provost marshal, Sandford Tennison. Loughton smiled more, at least he did on the few times Mason had seen him on the street. "Mister Jackson, too. You're both under arrest."

"Under arrest for what?" Charlie asked, as he assumed a defensive posture and attitude.

"Violating the trade laws," Sullivan said.

Mason, Jeremy, and Charlie stared at him with confused expressions.

"Smuggling. You've been running most of your crop up or down the coast."

"Which is it?" Mason asked. "Up or down the coast?"

"Remains to be determined," Loughton said. "An accusation has been made. There will be an inquiry and a trial, if warranted. For now, you'll both need to come with me for questioning."

The eyes of all the men in the group averted to something behind Mason.

He glanced back at Karen and Lisa approaching. Lisa held Michael, who was making gurgling sounds.

"What's going on?" Karen asked.

Mason took in a deep breath and exhaled. "The provost marshal here says Jeremy and I are under arrest. Says we've been smuggling rice."

"That's ridiculous," Lisa blurted.

Mason glanced at Sylvester and two other workers, standing a few feet away, and then turned back to Loughton. "It's alright. I'm sure Mister Loughton has proof of our wrong doing." He raised an eyebrow. "You do have some kind of proof, don't you? You're not here on a fishing expedition, right?"

"All in good time, Mister Mason," Loughton said. "For now, you'll need to come with me." He nodded at the four men behind him.

Since Mason had no intention of shooting his way out of this, it was lucky he had stopped wearing his

Glock in its shoulder holster around the plantation. It got in the way of work. Not having it now provided an additional benefit: if he were to be searched, the Glock would be a difficult thing to explain.

Mason held up his hand. "Not necessary, gentlemen. We'll come peacefully." He turned to Karen. "Could you grab my coat?"

Karen nodded, turned, and she and Lisa began walking toward the house with Michael still gurgling.

Mason looked at Charlie. "Take care of things while we're gone."

"Will do, Mason. Don't worry about a thing."

Mason put his arm around Charlie's shoulder and walked him a few feet away from the group. "Let Judge Trott know what's happening."

"You think this has something to do with Colonel Rhett? Him not being here to raise hell and all."

"Maybe," Mason said. "Just let Trott know. And let me know what he says."

"I will."

Mason began walking to meet Karen, returning with his coat. Lisa, no longer carrying Michael, walked beside her.

"I'm worried," Karen said, as she and Mason came together.

Lisa kept walking toward Jeremy.

"Don't be," Mason said. "Sullivan knows how much rice this land can produce and he knows he's not getting all of it. He's obviously the one behind the complaint. But he can't prove we've smuggled the balance unless he's been talking to Misses Stewart. And I doubt that's the case."

"Glad you're so confident," Karen said. "In this time period, they don't need much evidence to hang someone."

"You have a point. I've asked Charlie to let Judge Trott know." He raised his cheeks in a wince. "Not sure yet if that will help or hurt our case."

"This has to do with Colonel Rhett, doesn't it? They were out to get him. And now with him gone, and Trott having friends in London, you're the next best thing."

"Maybe," Mason said. "Or maybe it's because we treat our workers better than any other plantation. Could be anything. Except smuggling. No one in the colonies takes that violation seriously. It's a common practice." He took her in his arms. "I'll be back before you know it."

Karen exhaled. "Make sure you do just that."

They kissed.

"We're waiting, Mister Mason," Loughton said, standing next to his boat, a masted longboat.

Mason separated from Karen, winked, and then walked to the dock.

Jeremy and Lisa broke their embrace and he joined Mason.

Loughton stepped aboard first and made his way to the bow.

Sullivan followed and took a seat at the rudder.

Mason and Jeremy found seats while three of the four extra men manned the rowing stations.

The last man untied the line to the dock, stepped aboard, pushed off, and assumed his position as the fourth oarsman.

Mason and Jeremy stared at Karen and Lisa, still standing on the dock, as the oarsmen began churning the water. The current did most of the work. But even so, the oarsmen swept their long paddles while Sullivan steered.

"Where are we headed?" Jeremy asked Loughton. "The watch house?"

Mason had some experience with the watch house. It was a small, single-story brick structure near the wharves, at the intersection of Broad and Bay Streets. It was cramped, damp, and foul. The holding cell was bare of any furnishings, just three brick walls and a cobblestone floor. Months-old straw covered the stones. Occupants of the holding cell tended to stay put, despite the lack of any kind of door at the cell's wide entrance. The building was mainly the headquarters for the night watch, Charlestown's police force of sorts, along with an office for the provost marshal. The building's holding cell was often the final stop of the night for the drunk and disorderly. Mason did not relish the thought of spending time there.

"If I have your word as honorable gentlemen that you'll not try to escape, you'll be staying at my residence," Loughton said. He glanced at the sky. "It's late in the day. We'll go there directly. Do I have your word?"

Mason and Jeremy looked at each other.

"You do," Mason said.

Loughton looked at Jeremy.

Jeremy nodded his agreement.

Mason contemplated his response to what he imagined would be some rather direct questions. He glanced at Jeremy and found him deep in thought as well. They had not had time to formulate a common story. Perhaps now was a good time to start. He turned toward Loughton. "If this is about the amount of grain we send to market, there's a very simple explanation." Without giving Loughton a chance to shut him down, Mason continued, "We trade with the Indians. And we consume a great deal on the plantation. There's a way to turn rice into wine, but we're still working on the process."

"We obviously didn't want to release any of the details until the formula is perfected," Jeremy added.

"We figure wine would be more valuable than rice," Mason said.

Loughton glanced at Sullivan.

Sullivan cleared his throat. "Trading with the Indians and personal consumption wouldn't explain the absence of half your crop."

"We trade with a lot of Indians," Jeremy said.

"We've established a close bond with a group about seventy miles north of Charlestown," Mason added.

Sullivan opened his mouth to respond but Loughton cut him off.

"We can discuss this more once we talk to some witnesses," Loughton said. "We'll get to the truth. For now, just enjoy the hospitality I'm offering."

With that, everyone went quiet.

Mason gave a subtle nod to Jeremy and then lost himself in thought.

Once the boat entered the wide expanse of Charlestown harbor, the oarsmen stowed their oars and raised the sail. The sail cloth billowed, quickening the craft's pace through the water. Twenty minutes later, the boat bumped against the wharf nearest the watch house. The oarsmen scrambled out, secured the boat to the dock, and assisted the others as they disembarked.

Without a word, Sullivan and the four oarsmen peeled off as Loughton led Mason and Jeremy down Broad Street. They crossed over Church Street and turned south at the first side street, which was more of a wide alley. They passed several residential dwellings on both sides of the street.

Loughton finally stopped in front of a two-story, clapboard house with a wood slatted roof. It was much the same as the other houses on the street, narrow but deep. Most were constructed of unpainted wood, but Loughton's house was a light green on the first floor, and a pale white on the second. Both colors were thin, almost a whitewash that barely covered the wood grain. Three sets of windows looked out from the second floor; two windows and the front door on the ground floor. Three slender, wood pillars supported an overhang which protected a small porch.

The men's boots crunched in the oyster shell gravel as they walked to the front door.

Just as Loughton stepped onto the porch, the door swung open, revealing a black man in long pants, a blue long coat, and black leather shoes with silver buckles. "Welcome home, Mister William." The man's enunciation reflected near perfect English pronunciations and had obviously benefited from some form of education.

"Glad to be home, Alfred." He stopped on the porch and turned to Mason and Jeremy. "We have guests."

"Yes, sir, Mister William. The usual room?"

"That will be fine." He motioned for Mason and Jeremy to follow him inside.

They stepped through the threshold as Alfred held the door.

"Just follow Alfred. Everything you might need is in the room. He'll fetch you when dinner is ready."

His expression, and that of Alfred, indicated this was somewhat of a common occurrence. The fact that prisoners were held in the provost marshal's private home was something Mason never would have expected. And the man's hospitality was equally unexpected. Mason had no idea if he did this for all prisoners, just the ones he considered gentlemen, or just Mason and Jeremy. Whether it was a one-time thing or tradition, Mason wasn't complaining. Anything would be better than the watch house holding cell.

Without further comment, Alfred led Mason and Jeremy up a narrow set of stairs and down a short hall, to a room at the end. He opened the door and stepped to the side as he motioned for the two men to enter. "Dinner should be ready in an hour or so," he said in a neutral tone. With that he closed the door, leaving Mason and Jeremy inside the room alone.

The room contained two single beds, a straight-back chair, and a chamber pot. Both beds included a quilt over what was probably a straw mattress and a well-used, flat pillow. The only source of light was a single window providing a view of the area behind the house, basically an open field and the backs of other buildings beyond. Spartan, but the room was orderly and clean.

"What do you think?" Jeremy whispered.

"Nice enough room," Mason replied in a low tone.

"I mean about the charges against us."

"Just stick to our story, no matter what anyone says," Mason said, as he sat on one of the beds, pivoted, and reclined, keeping his boots over the edge and off the quilt. He intertwined his fingers behind his head as he stared at the tongue and groove ceiling. His eyes traced the lines between the ceiling and the bare plaster walls.

"You're just going to lie there?"

"Yeah. Until dinner."

"Glad to see you're taking this seriously," Jeremy said.

"Politics," Mason said. "Someone is trying to make a statement. For now, we listen, learn, and respond accordingly. It will all work out." Mason closed his eyes.

Jeremy took a seat on his bed and stared at Mason.

◆◆◆

"Tell me about your plantation," Misses Loughton said, as she placed a bowl of steaming stew in front of Mason. She wore the typical layers of petticoats, a short blouse, shoulder scarf, and a bonnet. With her auburn hair pulled into a tight bun, she was a remarkably attractive woman. She had the nicest teeth of anyone he had met in this time period, outside of Karen and Lisa. Part of that was likely due to her relatively young age, somewhere in her thirties.

Mason glanced at Mister Loughton at the end of the table, and Jeremy to his right, while Misses Loughton took a seat across from Jeremy. "A thousand acres which includes marsh, forest, and fields. We have about six hundred acres for the crops, but we're alternating our planting. Mostly rice." He peered at Mister Loughton. "That seems to be at the root of our current situation."

Loughton said nothing as he tore a hunk of bread in half and dipped a piece into his stew. He bit off the dripping corner and chewed as he stared at Mason.

"Well, I'm sure everything will work out for the best," Misses Loughton said. "How many slaves?"

Workers, he thought to himself. "Fifty."

"And the family?"

"Wife and one small child," Mason said. He looked at Jeremy. "And Jeremy and Lisa are family."

She turned her attention to Jeremy. "And you actually own the property."

"That's true, on paper," Jeremy said. "But like Mason said, the four of us are like family."

"You have a very nice home," Mason said, trying to change the subject. "A beautiful job on the plaster and wainscoting."

"William did a lot of the work himself," Misses Loughton said.

While everyone ate, Misses Loughton went into great detail describing the house and its construction. She talked about the furnishings. A few pieces were locally made, but most had been shipped from London.

Mason glanced around the dining room. He focused on the china displayed in a breakfront and the finely made furniture. There were even paintings on the walls. It occurred to Mason that the Loughton's lifestyle and possessions would not be possible on a provost marshal's income. There had to be an alternate source. Smuggling was the most likely candidate. A lot of people were involved in the practice, one way or the other.

CHAPTER 5

Mason's eyes blinked open to the sound of loud knocking on the front door of the Loughton house. He heard footfalls, the door opening, and the unmistakable voice of Judge Trott.

Jeremy rolled over to face Mason. "Sounds like Charlie got in touch with the judge."

"Sounds like it," Mason said, as he threw off the covers and slipped into his boots.

An overcast, early morning light filtered in through the window.

"Looks like rain."

"We can use the rain," Jeremy said, as he rose to a sitting position on the side of the bed. He slipped into his boots and followed Mason out the door and down the stairs.

Alfred, standing to one side of the open front door, came into view, followed by Mister Loughton walking in that direction. As Mason descended the stairs, Judge Trott came into view standing on the front porch. His back was to the open doorway. He spun around as Loughton came to a stop at the threshold.

"Morning, Judge. To what do I owe the pleasure?"

"You know why I'm here. You're holding Mister Mason and Mister Jackson. I represent them and I demand they be released immediately." He didn't shout, but he came close.

Mason stopped halfway down the stairs, not wanting to interrupt the exchange between the two men.

"Being held on suspicion of violating the navigation acts."

"That's ridiculous," Trott boomed. "No one in these parts gives a hill of beans about the King's navigation acts. That includes you."

"Maybe so, Judge, but my hands are tied. Sullivan convinced the governor, and here we are. I work at the pleasure of the governor."

"What evidence do you have?"

"There will be a trial, Judge. You're welcome to observe."

"When?"

"Not sure. Judge Smith wants to try a man being held for piracy first. He should be convening the admiralty court in a few days."

"I know Judge James Smith. He's a good man. Piracy, you say?"

"A member of Ned Low's crew. Drunk in Port Royal, he bragged about sailing with Low. The man was seized and brought here for trial. Joseph Libby is his name."

"That's all well and fine," Trott said, "what about Mason and Jeremy? Release them on their own recognizance, or release them to me."

"Can't do it, Judge. They'll have to remain in my custody until their trial."

"Can I talk to them?"

"I don't see where that would be a problem."

Both men turned to the sound of Mason and Jeremy continuing down the stairs.

"Judge Trott asked to speak to you gentlemen," Loughton said.

"Mind if we step outside with him?" Mason asked.

Loughton shook his head and motioned to the open door, which he closed behind them.

Trott turned, stepped off the porch, and started walking toward the street with Mason and Jeremy in tow.

The three men stopped at the edge of the gravel walkway.

"This is pure politics," Trott started. "Pure and simple. Sorry you boys have to be caught up in Governor Nicholson's games."

"We understand," Mason said, "but are they serious about holding a trial?"

"I think so," Trott said. "Trials are great entertainment for folks around here. And no matter the outcome, they send a message."

"What's the outcome likely to be?" Jeremy asked.

"You'll be acquitted. It would take a lot of evidence to convict a couple of landowners like yourselves."

"So, you think the governor put Sullivan up to making the accusation?" Jeremy asked.

"Yep," Trott replied. "Without a doubt. The two of them are thick as thieves. Literally."

"What about Loughton?" Mason asked.

"Good man. Fair."

"And the judge?"

"James Smith is fair as well."

"But we have to stay here?" Jeremy asked.

"For a few days," Trott said. "Smith has another trial first, a serious matter, likely to end in a hanging."

"We heard," Mason said. "Where are they holding this Joseph Libby? He's not here."

"Watch house, I imagine," Trott said. "They must have just brought him in, otherwise I would have already heard about him."

"And he was on Edward Low's crew?" Mason asked.

"That's what William just told me. Low has been running up and down the coast here for several months. I understand he has captured a great many merchantmen, from here to Boston. The navy has been in pursuit, but so far he's evaded all attempts at capture or destruction."

"I suppose authorities would like to see him captured or killed."

"Top priority," Trott said, "but why the interest in Ned Low?"

Mason took in a deep breath and exhaled. "We have a history." He glanced at Loughton's house. "Think they would let me talk to this Joseph Libby?"

Trott cocked his head and peered at Mason for several moments. He glanced at Jeremy and then turned his attention back to Mason. "Something happen between you and Low?"

"Let's just say, I'd like to have a few minutes with Mister Low. What about Libby?"

"I can ask," Trott said.

◆◆◆

Two men of the night watch supported a third man between them as they half carried and half dragged the limp carcass through the entrance to the watch building. With eyes closed, the man's head rolled from side to side as they moved.

"Another one for you," one of the watchmen said, as they stepped from the pitch dark into the interior, lit by a lantern on a table. Behind the table sat another member of the night watch.

The barrel-chested watchman stood as he flicked one hand toward the open holding cell. "In there."

The two watchmen carried the seemingly unconscious man to the back of the cell and let him drop.

The man *thumped* to the straw-covered floor and immediately curled into a ball on his side.

"He's alive," one of the watchmen said. "For now. Caught thieving and he assaulted Judge Trott. He'll be hanged in a day or two."

Another man, already in the cell, stirred, rolled to his back. Without opening his eyes, he scratched at his nose with hands tied with rope and quickly resumed his low, rumbling snore.

The other watchman kicked at the man they had brought in. "A double hanging, then."

"The sooner we can rid this building of their stench, the better," the barrel-chested watchman said.

The two watchmen exited the cell, spoke a few minutes with the man on duty for the night, and exited the building to resume their patrol.

The remaining watchman returned to his seat, leaned back, and lifted both his dirty boots to the top of the table.

◆◆◆

"How are you feeling this morning?"

The words registered, but just barely, as Forrest dug his way out of a deep sleep. He opened his eyes enough to see Karen hovering over him. He opened his eyes fully, rolled to his back, and pulled the covers tighter around his neck. "The best sleep in days, maybe weeks."

Karen touched his forehead with the back of her hand. "I believe you are fever free."

Forrest stared at Karen's face. "What's wrong?"

"That obvious?"

Forrest pushed himself to more of a sitting position and placed an extra pillow behind his head. "Tell me."

"They arrested Mason and Jeremy two days ago. Charged them with smuggling."

"Have they been smuggling?"

"Of course," Karen said, "but that's not really taken seriously in these parts. I suspect it's the same in New York."

"You're right. Everybody and their brother have something going on the side."

"Are you feeling well enough to get up? You could use a bath."

"I think so. Where's Mason right now?"

"The provost marshal took both of them. There's supposed to be an inquiry and then a trial, but there's been no word since they were taken. I expected to hear something by now."

"I'll go into town and see what I can find out," Forrest said, as he started to rise. He immediately sank back into the covers, for two reasons. He was weak as a kitten and he was still nude.

"One thing at a time. You'll feel better after a bath and something to eat." She lifted a thin robe from the back of a chair and tossed it on the bed. "Sylvester has been working on a warm bath for you. Should be ready. Can you get yourself out of bed and downstairs?"

"I think so," Forrest said.

Karen nodded, turned, and exited the room, closing the door behind her.

Forrest threw the covers back, slowly stood, and slipped into the robe. He made a pit stop at the chamber pot, and then made his way out of the room and down the stairs, supporting himself with walls and railings. He had not been on his feet in days and managing his own unsupported weight would take some time. As much as he wanted to check on Mason and Jeremy, going into town in his present condition would not be possible.

At the bottom of the stairs, Lisa stepped back several paces. She held young Michael in her arms. "Is he still contagious?"

Karen stepped into view and stood beside her. "I don't think so, but let's keep Michael away from him, just in case." She stepped forward, took Forrest's right arm, and draped it over her shoulders. "We're headed outside," she said, as she began guiding Forrest toward the back door. "It's cold outside, but only a few yards to the bathhouse."

"You have a bath house?"

"Bath and shower combo," she said. "We built two of them. One close to the main house and another one down near the worker's cabins. That one doesn't get a lot of use."

"Actually, I remember Mason saying something about bath or shower facilities. You're lucky if people in this era take a bath once a year."

"I know," Karen said, as she maneuvered him through the door. "And they think we're crazy for wanting a bath as much as we do. Just so they don't think we are totally crazy, we bathe once a week."

As they stepped onto the back porch, Karen motioned with her chin. "Kitchen and group dining area to the left, bath and shower to the right."

Forrest eyed the bath house. "A lot of wood. Looks like something that would be constructed for a sauna."

"It is a sauna in there during the summer."

"What's that on top?" He pointed to the wood construction with flared side panels erected on the roof.

"Catches the rain and stores it in a large barrel. Just turn the tap for a shower. Works like a beer keg. Water for a warm bath has to be heated over a fire. Mason and Jeremy usually just shower off with the cold water. Lisa and I insisted on a bathtub."

Despite the cold air, they walked slowly until they were at the three steps leading up to a thick, wooden door.

"Oak?" Forrest asked.

"The whole thing is made of solid oak," Karen said, as she opened the door. "Raised off the ground to give room for drainage." She helped Forrest navigate the three steps and the door.

Inside, Forrest stared at the structure. As Karen described, the end of a large barrel protruded partially through the flat roof. The wood spigot was within easy reach for an adult. He turned his attention to the bathtub, and admired the workmanship. It was constructed of oak slats, just like a barrel, except it was oblong, nearly as long and wide as a modern tub. Three steel straps banded the slats together just like a regular barrel. The far end of the tub, the head, was raised higher than the foot. He studied the round wood grate, about a foot in diameter, positioned directly under the shower. The entire room was steamy from the half-filled tub of warm water. "It's beautiful. It really does remind me of a sauna in a fancy men's club."

"Never been to one of those," Karen said, "but I understand what you're saying."

Forrest shuffled the few feet to a chair next to the tub and took a seat. He spotted his freshly laundered clothes folded on the seat of a three-legged stool against the wall.

"You need help getting in?"

He smiled and cocked his head. "As much as I'd like your help, I think I can manage."

"A true marine," she said with a slight smile.

"Always," Forrest said. "How long can I spend in here?"

"As long as you want." She handed him a bar of lye soap. "Scrub everything, especially your hair."

"Will do, madam."

◆◆◆

An hour later, Karen and Lisa sat across from a fully clothed Forrest at a table in the dining area off the kitchen. He spooned porridge into his mouth as the two women peppered him with questions about his life in 1945 Miami and in 18th century New York. Just as Forrest finished chewing and was about to answer another question, Jeremy stepped through the door.

Karen and Lisa jumped to their feet and rushed to him.

Lisa wrapped her arms around his waist and buried her head into his chest.

Karen looked through the open doorway. "Where's Mason?"

Jeremy tightened his lips, stared at Karen, and then finally spoke, "He's on a mission."

CHAPTER 6

"What do you mean?" Karen asked.

"I should start at the beginning," Jeremy said, as he nodded at Forrest and took a seat next to him. "You must be feeling better."

"I am," Forrest said, as he pushed the bowl of porridge back. "So, what happened to Mason?"

"Loughton took us to his home, where we ate and spent the night."

"Really?" Karen asked. "Not the watch house?"

At that moment, Charlie entered. He took a seat on the bench next to Lisa. "Gentlemen are apparently not held in the watch house."

Karen looked at Charlie with a knowing look, as though Charlie would know, given his inclination to overindulge.

Jeremy continued, "Judge Trott showed up yesterday morning."

"Said he would," Charlie said.

"Loughton refused to release us, but then he said something to Trott that got Mason's attention."

Four pairs of eyes peered at Jeremy expectantly.

Karen's patience broke first. "Yeah?"

"He told Trott that our trial would have to wait until the admiralty court considered another case. Apparently, they captured one of Ned Low's men in Port Royal and brought him here for trial."

"Ned Low?" Forrest asked.

"Notorious pirate," Karen said simply.

Forrest tossed both hands in the air.

"He's responsible for the death of people we knew," Jeremy said.

A knowing expression suddenly spread across Forrest's face. He glanced at Charlie, and then gave a slight nod to Jeremy.

"Plus, he kidnapped me," Lisa said, "but that's another story." She looked at Jeremy. "So, what's the mission?"

"Mason convinced Trott, who convinced Loughton to approach the admiralty judge and the governor about a deal." He paused for affect. "Let Mason befriend this prisoner, a Joseph Libby, and get Libby to trust him. Mason would hopefully be able to gather information about Low's whereabouts. Apparently, the authorities are much more interested in capturing Ned Low than they are in hanging Libby, at least for now."

"So, why did they release you?" Charlie asked.

"Dropped the charges on both of us and released me this morning. Part of the deal."

"Where's Mason?" Karen asked.

"They moved him to the watch house holding cell last night."

Karen bolted from her seat. "That's just like him," she yelled. "Run off on some half-cocked plan at revenge." She began pacing back and forth.

"What's the plan?" Forrest asked.

"Get close to Libby, get him to talk, and see where it leads," Jeremy said.

Karen stopped pacing. "If I know Mason, and I do, he has more in mind than just that."

"Just information," Jeremy said. "That's what he told me."

"What do we do?" Charlie asked.

"Glad you asked that, my friend. We're taking one of the sloops into town."

Karen started pacing again. "For what?"

"We stand by for a signal from Mason. We'll have to play it by ear."

"I'm coming too," Forrest said.

"You're in no condition to go traipsing off to who knows what," Karen said.

"I may not be in prime condition, but I can walk and I can fire a rifle."

❖❖❖

Mason dipped the stale bread into the bowl of lukewarm broth and munched on the now soggy corner. The taste was salty, but otherwise bland.

The man, with his back against the opposite wall, focused his full attention on getting his own broth and bread down his gullet as quickly as possible. It was a somewhat more involved task, with both hands still tied. Each of his swallows was immediately followed by another bite until the bread was gone. With both hands, the man then turned the bowl up to his lips and drank the remaining broth.

"I must have been a little under the weather when I came in last night," Mason said. "Don't remember much."

Without a word, and avoiding eye contact, the man slung his empty bowl to the straw next to his outstretched legs, pivoted, and reclined to his former sleeping position. He closed his eyes.

Mason placed his empty bowl on the straw, and on hands and knees he moved closer to the man. He leaned against the wall only a couple of feet from the man's head. "I can remove those ropes, if you want."

The man scrunched his nose when a fly landed on the very tip. The fly persisted until the man finally raised his hands to his face. The fly left but quickly returned to the same spot. He left for good when the man opened his eyes and went to a sitting position. He stared at Mason for several moments.

"Why would you want to do that?"

"Looks uncomfortable," Mason said. He glanced at the night watchman at the table just outside the holding cell and then motioned for the man to extend his hands. Mason was aware that there were always two men on duty, sometimes more, depending on the number of prisoners. The second watchman had stepped outside, probably for a latrine break.

The man's stench became even more apparent when Mason leaned in and untied the rope. "Name's Mason." Mason was aware that his own appearance and odor wasn't much better. Plus, he smelled of rum. The difference was that he had been purposefully made to look and smell the part.

"Libby," the man said. Rotten and broken teeth filled his mouth.

Libby never asked why Mason's hands weren't tied, and Mason saw no need to come up with an explanation.

"Assault on a judge is a hanging offense," Mason said. "But I don't plan on volunteering my neck for the gallows."

Libby's forehead wrinkled. For the first time he showed some interest in what Mason had to say.

At that moment two additional watchmen entered the building and went directly to the man at the desk. It was, Mason knew, time to change the guard.

Libby's interest in Mason instantly faded as he reclined back into his former prone position on the filthy straw. His hands now free.

Mason leaned closer. "We can take the two who will be left on duty," he whispered. "I need your help."

Without comment, Libby turned on his side and faced the wall.

Mason scrunched closer. "We'll both be dead in a couple of days if we don't do something."

"Get away from me or I'll kill you myself," Libby grumbled.

Mason leaned his back against the wall. "We have some time; just think about it."

◆◆◆

With Charlie and Forrest aboard the smaller and faster of the two sloops, Jeremy stood with Karen and Lisa at the foot of the dock.

"How will you know what Mason is up to?" Karen asked.

Jeremy took in a deep breath and exhaled while he twisted his lips. "He'll leave some kind of sign in the cell, if he's able. Otherwise, we'll just follow as best we can."

"How will he do that?" Lisa asked.

"I don't know, he'll find a way. He's supposed to make his move tonight, tomorrow night at the latest. We stand by, then follow."

Karen shook her head. "This is reckless. No real plan. Mason alone."

"We'll be close," Jeremy said. "Besides, I didn't have a choice. Mason was determined, and Loughton was all for a chance to get Ned Low." He put his hand on Karen's shoulder. "He'll be fine."

Karen stared at Charlie and Forrest making last minute preparations aboard the sloop. "You have everything you need?"

"Plenty of food and water. Enough for a couple of weeks, if needed. We have the flintlocks and plenty of cartridges. And you have Mason's Glock. Don't be afraid to use it."

"Don't worry about us," Karen said. "Worry about yourselves."

"We'll bring him back."

"And make sure Forrest takes the antibiotics. A few more days should do it."

Jeremy nodded as Karen turned and started walking toward the house. Jeremy wrapped his arms around Lisa.

"Just be careful," she said. She kissed him, turned, and walked away, leaving Jeremy to peer after her.

He finally turned, sauntered down the dock, and jumped aboard the sloop. "Forrest, if you'll man the rudder, Charlie and I will handle the polling."

Two hours later, in the late afternoon, Jeremy tied off the bow and stern lines to an open spot at a dock, a hundred yards down from the night watch building. "Stay with the boat," he said to Charlie and Forrest. He saw Loughton walking in his direction down the wharf. "I'll check in with the provost marshal."

The two men met midway.

"Anything?" Jeremy asked.

"The two of them were talking," Loughton said. "Mason released him from his ropes. That's about it."

"Do the night watchmen on duty know not to shoot either of them?"

"They do. And they know to follow Mason's lead."

Jeremy looked up and down the wharves. "Your longboat?"

Loughton pointed to a dock directly in front of the watch house. "Ready and easily accessible. Mason knows where it is."

"Won't that seem awfully convenient?"

"It's what Mason wanted."

"The plan is still for Mason to lead Libby to the boat and get him alone out on the water."

"You were there when Mason came up with this idea," Loughton said. "He thinks Libby will be more forthcoming if Mason helps him escape."

"Any idea where Low is?" Jeremy asked.

"Not precisely. He's been marauding up and down this coast for months now. We know he was in Port Royal a week ago. What we don't know is whether Libby jumped ship or was on a fact-finding mission of some sort. If it's the latter, Low will be back to retrieve him."

"So, we wait," Jeremy said.

"It'll be at night, maybe tonight."

"There may not be time to check in with you. If we see them, we'll pursue at a safe distance."

"I understand," Loughton said.

The two men parted and Jeremy returned to the sloop.

"What did he say?" Forrest asked.

"Nothing, so far. We'll keep watch from here. If we see them come out, we'll follow."

"Shifts?" Charlie asked.

"Yeah."

◆◆◆

Dim light from the lantern next to the watchmen threw long shadows in Mason's holding cell. He glanced at Libby, still on his side against the wall. He had not stirred since sundown.

The two watchmen huddled over the table deep in conversation about a new tavern that had just opened in town. It had been hours since either of them had taken a latrine break. One or the other would be stepping out eventually.

Mason leaned over Libby and shook his shoulder. "The next time one of them leaves, I'm out of here. You coming or not?" he whispered.

Libby pushed Mason's hand away with his own, but otherwise did not move or speak.

Mason exhaled and leaned back. It was like Libby was waiting for something. At that point, Mason decided he would have to wait with him. Let Libby make the first move.

◆◆◆

With the moon and stars bright against the night sky, Jeremy rolled to his back on the makeshift bed. He tossed the blanket to the side and got to his feet next to the tiller. He saw Charlie's silhouette at the bow.

"Anything?" Jeremy asked, as he eased up next to Charlie.

"Nothing."

"You should probably get some sleep."

Charlie's chin, barely visible in the dark, lifted. He turned toward the stern.

At that moment, Jeremy saw movement, something on the water off to his right. He heard the soft thud of wood against wood. "Hold up," he whispered. He raised his hand in the direction of the sound.

Charlie turned back and peered in that direction. He studied the darkness for several moments and listened to more dull thuds. "Oars," he whispered back. "A longboat."

They watched as the boat quietly glided through the water and came to rest against a dock farther down the wharf, halfway to the watch house.

Jeremy and Charlie watched as five men, their bodies silhouetted against the slightly lighter sky, climb out of the boat. All five started off toward the watch house.

"This, we were not expecting," Charlie said, just barely audible.

"What is it?"

"They're going to break their man out," Charlie said.

Jeremy placed a boot on the gunwale and started to rise up.

Charlie pulled him back down by his coat tail. "Mason said to be prepared for anything and don't intervene unless absolutely necessary."

"But—"

"He said to follow his lead."

Jeremy put his boot back down on the deck. He took a deep breath and exhaled.

CHAPTER 7

Mason's eyes popped open at the sound of gravel crunching underfoot, just outside the watch house door. The sound was subtle but unmistakable. He shifted his gaze to the two watchmen. One was leaned back in a straight-back chair, sound asleep. The other was awake, but just barely. Mason watched his head bob back and forth as he fought to stay awake.

The man came wide awake when the door opened and a rather ragged looking man stepped in.

Mason saw that he held a flintlock pistol in his outstretched hand and was followed by four other men, two armed with pistols and two with daggers. All five wore breeches and shirts, grubby and stained. Three wore long coats, including the lead man. This man also wore a second pistol stuffed in his waistband, and a cutlass on his hip. His hair was long, black, and straggly, capped with a three-pointed hat. Mason recognized him immediately. Ned Low. Mason's last image of Low—standing on the deck of his schooner—flashed into his mind. It was the last thing Mason saw before a cannon ball blasted him and his sloop's mast into the water all those months ago.

Low glanced at the open holding cell and tightened his lips at the sight of Libby getting to his feet.

"About time," Libby said, as he joined his compatriots.

The watchman that had been asleep awakened and rocked forward. The front two legs of his chair slammed to the floor.

The other watchman eyed the flintlock pistol on the table, only a foot from his hand. He looked at Mason, still sitting in the holding cell, and back to the pistol. He moved his hand farther away, so there would be no mistaking his intention.

One of Low's men stepped forward. "What about the watchmen?"

"What about them?" Low replied, as he shoved his pistol into his waistband next to the second pistol. He withdrew a long, slender-bladed knife from a scabbard. "They're not bothering us, why should we bother them?"

Both watchmen visibly relaxed.

"It would be best," Low said, "if we get in and get out. That was the plan. We have what we came for. Mostly." He smiled as he stepped behind the closest watchman's chair. He put one hand on the man's shoulder. He moved his hand to the top of the watchman's head, grasped a handful of the man's hair, and jerked his head back. Without skipping a beat, he brought the knife across the man's neck, leaving a thin, red line. The line thickened and quickly gushed with blood, which flowed down the man's chest.

The second watchman's eyes widened to the size of saucers. He eyed the pistol again.

Before his hand had moved an inch, Low flicked his wrist, driving the thin blade through the man's temple. The watchman's body went limp. When Low withdrew the blade, the man's torso fell forward. His head bounced once and then settled on the tabletop.

Mason instantly felt sick to his stomach. This was his plan. He was responsible for the death of the watchmen. He vomited.

Low's man closest to the holding cell peered into the relative darkness at Mason. "What about him?" he asked, as he motioned with the pistol in his hand.

"What about him?" Low asked, as he wiped the blade of his knife on the watchman's back. He ambled a few steps toward the cell, stopping next to Libby. "Who's your friend?"

"In here for thieving. Said he assaulted a judge."

Low rocked his head up and down and continued into the cell until he stood peering down at Mason. "That true?"

Mason looked up at Low, but said nothing. He kept his expression neutral but, inside, the hate he felt for the man towering over him had just multiplied exponentially. The man would die, even if Mason died doing it. He moved both hands from his lap to the straw at his thighs. Imperceptibly, he flexed the muscles in his forearms and biceps readying himself to spring forward. He had no doubt he could strip the knife from Low's hand and drive it into his groin before he knew what had happened.

A millisecond before Mason pounced, Low turned away and began walking. "Bring him."

Two of Low's men each took an armpit and raised Mason to his feet. One gave him a hard shove to the middle of his back, in the direction of Low, already leading the way through the watch house door.

Mason stepped into the darkness surrounded by Low, Libby, and the four other men and was roughly herded toward the wharves.

◆◆◆

Jeremy and Charlie watched as the group of men reemerged into view from the side of the watch house. Jeremy counted seven silhouettes. The two extra men had to be Mason and Libby.

The seven men walked out onto the dock and climbed down to their waiting longboat.

"Keep an eye on that boat," Jeremy said, as he put a foot on the gunwale. "And get the sloop ready to leave." He leapt to the dock and scurried down the wood planks, using boats and rigging for cover. Keeping to the shadows, he ducked around the side of the watch house, made his way along the north wall, and into the front entrance. Dull, flickering candlelight danced on the surfaces, giving the interior an eerie glow. He did a double-take at the two watchmen, both motionless, with their blood-covered heads on the table. The only sound was the *splat* of the red, viscous liquid as it dripped from the table and hit the floor.

He stepped back outside and looked around for any other soul. He saw one, a man stumbling along Bay Street on his way from an obvious night of drinking. Jeremy dashed the forty yards to the man, grabbed him by the sleeve of his coat, and half dragged him back to the watch house. He pulled the man inside the doorway. "Open your eyes and look," he said with a stern voice.

The man wobbled a bit, squinted his eyes, and then turned to leave as a look of realization spread across his face.

Jeremy turned the man back around to face the two dead watchmen. "Go now and wake up William Loughton. The provost marshal. Don't go home and don't go to sleep. Go straight to Loughton's home. Do you understand?"

The man's head rocked up and down.

"Tell him what has happened here. And tell him Jeremy saw five men enter and seven men exit. They have Mason and I'm in pursuit."

"Who are you?" the man slurred.

"Jeremy. I'm Jeremy. Remember, five men in, seven men out. They have Mason, and I'm in pursuit. You got it?"

"I do," the man said, as he suddenly became more alert.

Jeremy, still holding the man's sleeve, dragged him back to the door and gave him a shove. "Go now."

The man shuffled off to the south on Bay Street.

Jeremy rushed back to the table and grasped the flickering candle. Using it to light the way, he entered the holding cell. He wrinkled his nose at the stench, which had suddenly gone up a few notches in intensity. He extended the candle as he searched along the walls for any sign Mason might have left. He scraped at the straw with his foot, searched the walls again, and then hurried out of the cell. He replaced the candle, dashed out the door, and low trotted back to the sloop.

"Anything?" Charlie asked, as Jeremy jumped back aboard.

"Both watchmen are dead," Jeremy said. "Mason and Libby are gone."

Charlie's eyes went wide a few moments before he subtly shook his head. With lips tight, he exhaled through his nose as he pushed off from the dock and manned the tiller.

The forward hatch creaked open and Forrest stuck his head up through the opening. "What's happening?" he whispered.

"Mason and Libby are gone, the watchmen are dead, and we're tailing the men who murdered them."

"Any sign from Mason?" Forrest asked, as he climbed on deck.

"Didn't see anything. I'm guessing he didn't have time, or wasn't given any indication where they were going. Probably both."

Forrest stood up and examined his surroundings. "What are we pursuing?"

"Longboat," Jeremy said. "They'll meet up with their ship farther out. We have time to find them and decide the best course."

When the Cooper River's current had carried them into open water, Jeremy raised the mainsail while Charlie steered.

Forrest kept his eyes peeled from the bow.

When the sail billowed with the light onshore breeze, Charlie steered east, then southwest, and then back to the east in a zigzag toward the open mouth of Charlestown harbor.

"Anything?" Jeremy asked, as he joined Forrest in the bow.

"Nothing, but there's not a lot of light. We might be on top of them before we know it."

"Keep looking," Jeremy said, as he turned and began making his way aft.

"Where we headed?" Charlie whispered when Jeremy was in earshot.

Jeremy stared out at the darkness while he slowly inhaled and exhaled. He finally shook his head. "Don't have a clue. Let's just head for open water, and then beyond the coast a couple of miles. We'll wait for something to show up."

"And then what?"

Jeremy shook his head again. "Don't have a clue about that either."

◆◆◆

Killing Ned Low would be easy, Mason thought. *Getting away with it unscathed would be the trick.* That's what Mason was thinking as he followed Low up the outside hull of the single-masted sloop. Mason had no doubt he could snap the man's neck before he knew what was happening. That's what Mason wanted to do. He even pictured the sequence in his mind. But now wasn't the time, not while he was surrounded by so many armed men.

As Mason stepped onto the deck, in near total darkness, he scanned his surroundings. A few twinkling lights, probably campfires in and around Charlestown, were visible in the distance to the west. A tree line, barely visible against the eastern sky, was much closer. Mason figured the sloop was anchored in that part of the harbor between Sullivan's Island, and what would become Mt. Pleasant. As casually as possible, he surveyed the darkness toward

Charlestown for any sign that Jeremy might be near. He saw nothing.

"Lash him to the mast for now," Low said to the man standing next to Mason. With no further comment, he turned and headed aft, toward the helm. "Weigh anchor," he said to no one in particular, "and get us moving. Want to be well away before the sun."

Two men each grabbed an arm and guided Mason to the base of the mast. They pushed him into a sitting position and tied both hands with a length of rope wrapped around the mast.

He watched as men moved about the deck quietly. He heard the sounds associated with the windlass being cranked to raise the anchor. Several men, using a block and tackle affixed to the boom, raised the longboat and positioned it on deck, just behind the mast.

Two men approached where Mason sat. One put a boot within an inch of where Mason rested his hand on the deck. Together they pulled a line which raised the yoke of the gaff-rigged mainsail.

Soon, the ship slowly began to move, to the west at first, but soon to the south, in the direction of open water.

Mason stared at the twinkling lights of Charlestown as the boat came around. He wondered if he had made a gigantic miscalculation in his plan to locate and neutralize Ned Low. His doubt likely accounted for the mass of butterflies in his stomach.

He couldn't see much in the dark, but he had a general feel for the vessel upon which he sat. The single mast told him this was a sloop. But the distance between the mast and the helm's tiller in the stern, and the six cannons lined up along each hull, told him this sloop was much larger than either of his own sloops. He was on the main deck, the gun deck. Given the size of the boat, actually a ship in this case, there would be a second deck below, and a bilge below that.

This was not the same vessel Low used to attack Mason and the airline survivors three years earlier. That had been a schooner, an even larger ship.

"We'll rendezvous with Ranger off Royal," Mason heard Low say from the helm. Apparently, he now commanded at least two vessels with which to menace commercial shipping. There was no wonder Loughton was highly motivated to stop him.

 Mason rested his head back against the mast and stared up at the stars. He contemplated his options. Only one plan entered his mind. *Get loose, kill Low, and escape.* There was no plan B. He took in a deep breath and exhaled as he stretched the muscles in his neck and shoulders. He closed his eyes, cleared his mind, and let it go numb.

A sudden jolt that reverberated along the entire length of the sloop jostled Mason awake. Morning, but just barely. The sun, to his left, was peeking over the horizon. They were headed northeast, with moderate winds off the beam. The ship crashed against a wave and Mason felt the same jolt as before. He tried to scratch an itch on his cheek but immediately felt the constraint of the rope.

"Need to piss," he said to a man scurrying along the deck.

The man glanced at Mason but continued aft without a pause.

"I said I need to take a piss," Mason yelled.

His voice caught the attention of Low, still standing at the tiller.

"Let him loose," Low said to the man closest to Mason. "And put him to work. Deck needs scrubbing."

The man approached and stood over Mason. He wore a tattered, white long-sleeve shirt and what had been white, long pants at one time but now were stained highwaters with a ragged hem. Something resembling black slippers covered his feet. He pulled a long, curved dagger from a scabbard on his hip and waved it in front of Mason's face. He smiled, winked, and then began sawing through the rope.

Pain shot through Mason's shoulders as the stretched tendons suddenly released and retracted. He rolled both shoulders to get the blood flowing before he got to his feet. Without waiting for permission, he hurried to the bow against a bucking deck, unbuttoned the flap to his breeches, and urinated over the side.

Finished, Mason turned to the man at his side. "I could use something to drink."

The man laughed. "Says he could use something to drink," he yelled loud enough for Low to hear.

Low nodded. "Give him some grog, a biscuit, and put him to work."

CHAPTER 8

Captain Peter Solgard stood ramrod straight at the helm with his hands clasped behind his back. He gazed up into the rigging of the three-masted frigate and admired the square sails as they billowed with the wind. His eyes returned to the main deck and followed various crew members as they went about their business. Duties were plentiful, even with a crew of a hundred and thirty. The royal ship HMS Greyhound, a sixth rate, was not a ship-of-the-line, but a fine command just the same. With its twenty cannons, all nine-pounders, the ship had already proven itself a worthy combatant.

"Tell me what you're thinking, Mister Smith."

Lieutenant Edward Smith, the ship's second in command, pivoted his equally straight frame in order to face the captain.

Both men were dressed similarly with navy-blue long coats, white waistcoats and shirts with ruffled cuffs, white breeches and hose, black shoes, and a three-pointed hat. Both coats and hats were trimmed with gold braid, but more so on the captain's coat. Neither would qualify as a uniform, not officially. Royal Navy uniforms wouldn't be standardized for another twenty-five years. But the clothes identified the two men as upper class, and officers of His Majesty's ship.

"The Carolinas," Smith said.

Solgard glanced at Long Island's thin strip of white sand, astern in the distance. "Maybe, but I think we'll head north for now. Make it so, Mister Smith."

Smith leaned to the helmsman at the wheel. "Nor-nor-east."

The man turned the wheel to the left. Nothing happened at first, but after a few moments the large three-decked vessel began coming around.

Smith took a few steps forward and cupped both hands around his mouth. "The sails, Master Scott," he yelled.

The ship's master wasn't a royal officer per se, but he was responsible for the deck and ensuring the right amount of sail was deployed for the conditions, and that they were trimmed.

"Aye, Mister Smith."

Scott immediately directed men to the necessary lines. Scott was in his late thirties, slender, with a short, red beard, and no mustache. He wore long white pants, a reddish waistcoat over a white linen shirt, a kerchief tied around his neck, and a short, blue coat, the hem stopping just above the waist, open at the front. And he wore a brimmed hat cocked to one side. It could almost have passed for a uniform of sorts, except for its ruffled and wrinkled appearance.

"Thank you, Mister Smith," Solgard said. "Notify me of any sightings."

Smith nodded. "Of course, sir."

Solgard spun on his heels, stepped into the overhang, past the ladder leading to the quarter deck, and opened the door to the great cabin, which served as the captain's cabin and the officer's meeting room. It was also where he took dinner with most of his officers nearly every night. On this particular cruise, his officers included three lieutenants, two acting lieutenants, and five midshipmen. All were expected to attend the captain's mess when invited, except those on duty.

He walked directly to the stern windows and placed his forearms on the sill of the center opening. He stared at the coastline of New York as it faded into the distance. His wife's image, holding their small child, passed through his mind, but his thoughts quickly turned to his mission. *Locate Edward Low and eliminate his ability to attack shipping along the coast.* Solgard was authorized to sail as far north as Nova Scotia and as far south as the border with Spanish Florida. Based on reports from a number of ship's captains menaced by the pirate in recent weeks, he could be anywhere along that coast.

◆◆◆

"Sails ho!" the lookout in the crow's nest yelled.

Mason paused his scrubbing and popped his head above the gunwale. He saw nothing but water from his lower elevation in the bow. He glanced at the man in the crow's nest and looked again in the direction the man was pointing. He saw nothing at first, but then his eyes caught movement on the horizon. A tiny triangle of white. A sloop, or perhaps a schooner.

"It's the Ranger," the man in the crow's nest yelled.

Mason saw Low lean toward the helmsman and say something Mason couldn't hear.

The helmsman pushed on the tiller and, a few moments later, Mason felt the ship make a slight course change. He focused on the triangle of white until he suddenly felt the presence of someone close by. He swiveled his head and found Low staring down at him.

"What's your name?" Low asked.

Mason hesitated while he rose to his feet, trying to think of whether Low might already have heard his real name. He thought of the four men from Low's crew that he and Charlie fought on the beach, years earlier, when Spriggs kidnapped Lisa. He had left them alive, contrary to Charlie's advice at the time. That was unfortunate, and it was something Mason hadn't considered when he hatched the idea to find Low. But then, he didn't expect to actually end up on Low's ship. If any of those four men were on this vessel or the Ranger, that might be a problem. Mason's name might have been mentioned during the altercation but, more likely, Mason would be recognized. But it was a little late to worry about that now.

"Do you have a name?" Low grunted.

"Mason. People call me Mason."

"Mason, have you ever crewed a ship?"

"I've had some experience," Mason said.

"You've had some experience," Low repeated as he squinted. "That's an interesting answer. Not sure if it means yes or no."

Mason said nothing.

"Enough scrubbing," Low said. "Join the crew. Work hard, fight hard, and you'll share in the bounty."

Again, Mason said nothing. He dropped the brush he had been holding to the deck and simply raised his chin.

Low gave a single nod as he turned toward the helm. "Put him to work on the lines when the time comes," he said to a man standing nearby.

"Aye, Ned," the man responded.

Mason glanced at the man and then back to the approaching triangle of white, now recognizable as a sloop. He scanned the water in all directions for any other vessels or land in sight. There was none of either, but he knew he was likely approaching the Port Royal area. All he could remember of this time in history, about Ned Low, was that he marauded shipping from one end of the Atlantic to the other. For now, he would just have to go along until an opportunity presented itself.

◆◆◆

"What now?" Charlie asked, as he stood in the stern with his hand on the tiller.

Jeremy and Forrest stood next to him. Both men were focused on the mouth of Charlestown harbor in the morning sun. For hours they had sailed back and forth, well off shore, watching for any vessels leaving the harbor. There had been none that they saw.

"Think they got past us in the dark?" Forrest asked.

"Had to," Jeremy said. He rubbed his face with one hand as he stared at the deck. "Any ideas?"

"They caught Libby in Port Royal," Charlie said.

"But they have Libby, why would they go back there?" Forrest asked.

Jeremy continued staring at the deck for several moments longer but finally looked up. "It's all we have. We head northeast."

Charlie motioned for Forrest to take the tiller and then stepped off toward the mast.

"What do we know about this pirate?" Forrest asked.

"Edward Low was the worst of the worse," Jeremy said, with a grim expression. "He not only kills with wanton disregard; he maims and tortures for the fun of it. That's about all I know of the man."

"That's enough," Forrest said. "Haven't known you guys that long; you and Mason seem very capable, but one man going after a boatload of pirates. I'm not seeing the logic."

"Mason just wanted information from Libby. At least initially. I don't think he had a plan beyond that, other than relay that information to the authorities and then maybe participate in some way."

"No plan survives first contact with the enemy," Forrest said.

Jeremy nodded. "Apparently true, no matter how simple the plan."

◆◆◆

"Reduce sail and bring us alongside, Mister Thomas," Low said to the man standing next to him.

The man was younger than Low, taller, and even more ominous, if that was possible. Both had dark, penetrating eyes. Apparently, this was Low's first mate.

The man walked forward and gave the appropriate commands.

Without hesitation, the men scurried, the main and the jib were reduced, and the helmsman steered for the approaching sloop. Soon both sloops were side-by-side.

A younger man, early twenties, with an air of confidence, stepped to the gunwale of the Ranger. He was thin, dressed in a long sleeve linen shirt and long pants tucked into high black boots. His long, black hair was tied in a ponytail reaching to the middle of his back. He carried a flintlock pistol tucked in his waistband and a cutlass on his hip. He was apparently the Ranger's captain. "Any problems?"

"In and out," Low said.

It occurred to Mason that Low had gone to a lot of trouble to rescue Libby. He was just one man, and he didn't seem all that important among the crew.

"Libby?"

Low lifted his chin. "Come aboard, Mister Harris. We need to talk."

A light went on in Mason's head. *Charles Harris.* He was nearly as notorious as Low himself. According to what Mason had read, there were actually three of them working together: Charles Harris commanding the Ranger, Low with his sloop, and Francis Spriggs. Spriggs was the one who kidnapped Lisa from the plantation. Mason couldn't remember all the details about the three men, but he seemed to remember that Low's schooner, the Fancy, was still in the picture, presumably commanded by Spriggs. That gave Low three ships in his little armada. Mason had no idea where Spriggs and the Fancy were at the moment, but he was relieved they were not here. Those able to recognize Mason were more likely aboard the Fancy, with Spriggs.

Harris climbed aboard and followed Low through a hatch at the stern.

Mason presumed that, as a member of the crew, he could now roam freely. Since he hadn't had the opportunity to explore below deck, he figured now was a good time to start. He scanned the deck and saw that most of the crew were lounging or conversing with members of the other ship. He stepped through the hatch opening forward of the mast, down the ladder, and onto the deck below. It turned out to be a long, open deck crammed with barrels and sacks of goods apparently pilfered from commercial ships. A small galley occupied most of the forward section of the ship, and hammocks hung throughout. There were several crew members about, two in the galley, working on the next meal apparently, and the rest scattered along the length of the deck. Some were working to secure the cargo. Mason made his way along the deck aft, toward the stern, until he came to a solid bulkhead. He could hear muffled voices from the other side, but there did not appear to be an entrance to that section from the cargo deck. Apparently, the only entrance was from the hatch in the stern on the upper gundeck.

He stepped closer to the bulkhead and bent over as though looking for something. He tried to focus on the voices. But the sounds were too muffled to hear what was being said. He stood up and made his way back along the deck, up the forward ladder, and to the bow of the gundeck. He began coiling a line, trying to look busy. With that done, he began working his way along the deck with menial tasks—a little tidying here, a little restacking there—until he was next to Libby, attending to one of the port guns. "Thank you for helping me escape from Charlestown."

Libby gave a slight nod without looking up from his work.

"What do you think they're talking about down there?"

Libby glanced at the stern hatch and then refocused on his work without a reply.

"I ask because I'm just wondering where we're headed."

"That's simple," Libby muttered. "Where Ned decides."

"Yeah, but you must have some idea. He sent you to Royal to gather information, right?"

Libby said nothing as he continued to work.

"What did you find out?"

"North," Libby said.

"North?"

"I 'spect we're heading north," Libby said, as he stood up and moved to the next cannon. "New York."

Mason went quiet until another crew member walked past and was out of earshot. "What's in New York?"

"Treasure ship."

Mason cocked his head. He had never heard of an English treasure ship in the colonies. There was no gold or silver to speak of. Colonial merchants generally bought their merchandise on credit from London, and then repaid the debt with raw goods, like grain or tobacco. Raw goods were shipped to London in exchange for finished goods. The Crown took a share of the raw goods as tax, in accordance with the Navigation Acts which were enacted in the middle seventeenth century. "What treasure?"

Libby pulled a clay smoking pipe from a pouch tied at his waist. The pipe had a small bowl and a short stem. With no fire handy to light tobacco, the bowl remained empty as he stuck the stem into his mouth and held it with his discolored and chipped teeth. He leaned back against the gunwale as he studied Mason's face.

"There's no gold or silver."

"Merchant debt," Libby said, as he removed the pipe from his mouth and jabbed the stem at Mason's chest. "Paid in specie coin to the London debtors."

"Not sure I understand," Mason said.

"Not many know," Libby said, "but around this time each year, the New York merchants pay the balance due on their debts. If the balance ain't settled, they get no more credit. Mostly paid in coin collected during the year."

"And you learned this in Port Royal?"

"Naw, common knowledge," Libby mumbled, as he stuck the pipe stem back into his mouth. "But I heard 'bout when the ship is to depart, and which ship. People talk."

"Out of New York?"

"Yep. People from all over pass through Royal."

"Which ship and when?"

"A brig. Don't know the name. Departing sometime in a week or so."

"And we'll be intercepting this brig?"

Libby nodded as he placed the pipe back inside the pouch. He returned to his work without further comment.

Mason now understood why Low took the risk to retrieve Libby from the Charlestown watch house. A cache of actual coins provided a powerful incentive. Mason placed both hands on the gunwale and stared at the open ocean.

CHAPTER 9

Charlie suddenly turned from his perch in the bow and scurried aft, to the helm.

"Two ships coming into view," Charlie said. "Sails down. They're side-by-side." He pointed in the direction of their current heading.

Jeremy jerked his head from side to side trying to catch a glimpse past the mainsail and jibs. Just as Charlie said. The hulks of two ships were about eight miles out, just visible on the horizon. Jeremy was able to make out the naked masts of both ships. "What do you think?"

"I think it's Ned Low. Single masted, armed sloops. At least twice the size of this boat."

"What's going on?" Forrest asked, as he joined the two men at the helm.

"Ships," Jeremy said. "Might be our guys."

Forrest jerked his head where Charlie pointed.

"He's known to have two or three ships," Charlie said. "Sloops. Those ships match the description."

Forrest stared in the direction of the sloops for several moments. "Why would they be stopped in the middle of the ocean?"

"Don't know," Charlie said. "Conference maybe."

"Makes sense," Jeremy said. "They have Libby—"

"And Mason," Charlie added.

"Libby and Mason," Jeremy continued. "Conferring, planning their next move."

"Mason is on one of those ships," Charlie said confidently.

"What do we do?" Forrest asked.

Jeremy glanced up at the sails. "We slow down. Don't want to run up on them." He looked at Charlie. "Reef the mainsail."

Charlie immediately stepped off toward the mast.

"This boat offers a much smaller silhouette," Jeremy said. "We should be able to keep them in sight without becoming too obvious."

"Keep our distance, keep pace, and trail behind," Forrest said. "Remind me again, what are we watching for?"

"I don't know. Something odd."

"This is already odd," Forrest said.

Jeremy smirked. "We just need to keep them in sight and be ready to help Mason when the opportunity arises."

"They will be attacking something sooner or later. What do we do then?"

Jeremy rubbed the back of his neck. "Not much we can do. Just keep an eye on them."

Forrest shook his head but said nothing. After inhaling and exhaling deeply, he moved off to give Charlie a hand.

◆◆◆

Low and Harris emerged through the deck hatch from what was apparently the captain's cabin.

Mason watched as they continued their conversation. Suddenly, the talking stopped and Low scanned the deck until his eyes latched onto the man standing near Mason.

"Libby," he said, as he motioned for Libby to approach.

As Libby ambled in their direction, Mason slid a few feet closer, to within hearing distance.

"Harris needs a first mate," Low said, as Libby came to a stop before the two men. "You're elected."

Libby started to speak, but Low cut him off.

"We'll be taking on a few of his crew since we're short manned."

Libby simply nodded in agreement.

"Prepare the Ranger to get underway," Harris said. He lifted a chin at Low and followed Libby over the gunwales to the waiting Ranger.

After five men from the Ranger boarded Low's sloop, he turned to the helmsman. "Keep the Ranger in sight. We'll be holding fast off New York."

"Aye," the helmsman responded.

Low motioned for his men to get the ship underway. He then focused on Mason. "The sails, if you will, Mister Mason."

Mason went directly to the mast and, with the help of another man, began tugging on the mainsail halyard.

The mainsail's yoke and gaff began their track up the mast, pulling the white sailcloth along as they rose.

Ranger's sails caught the wind first and began pulling away.

Mason secured the halyard to an open belaying pin on the pin rail at the base of the mast and coiled the excess line, which he looped over the exposed length of the same pin.

Other men secured the two jib and single mainsheets.

The large ship began moving and took up a position two hundred yards behind Ranger as the two ships headed off to the northeast.

Mason contemplated the elephant in the room: what should he do, what could he do, when Low attacked his next merchant vessel? Could he stand by and do nothing while Low and his men slaughtered merchantmen crew members? It would be him against an armed crew of twenty-five men. In the chaos of battle, Mason could probably take out Low. But it was a near certainty the crew would exact revenge. They were generally loyal that way, at least from what he had seen so far. It was a dilemma, and one Mason was sure he would be facing in the near future.

◆◆◆

"They're moving to the northeast," Charlie said, loud enough for Jeremy and Forrest to hear.

"Can we keep up with them?" Forrest asked Jeremy, as the two men stood at the helm.

"Copper bottom and plenty of sail," Jeremy replied, "we can keep up."

Forrest shook his head. "I just don't see how we're supposed to keep them in sight, night and day, from this far away. Plus, we're too far to do any good if Mason needed our help, even if we knew he needed our help."

"All good points, Forrest. Any ideas how we solve any of those problems?"

Forrest stared off into the distance at the two pirate ships. He glanced at Charlie, standing in the bow. "Two guys from the future chasing pirates on the open sea." He shook his head and then turned to Jeremy. "That's just crazy. This has to be the most elaborate dream ever."

"I wish it were," Jeremy said. "Nothing would please me more than to wake up in my own time, in my own bed."

"Just out of curiosity, did you know Lisa in your previous life?"

"Nope, met her after we crashed in the ocean. And even in our little group of survivors, she and I together kind of defies logic."

"How's that?"

"She's nearly fifteen years my senior," Jeremy said.

"She doesn't look it," Forrest said. "So how did that happen?"

"After the other survivors ran into Ned Low, it was just the four of us, five if you count Nathan."

"I can see how it might have made sense for the two of you to join up," Forrest said. "I remember Nathan. Met him that one time. I guess on your first trip to New York. Mason never said exactly what happened to him. Except that he died. Seemed like a nice enough guy."

Jeremy snorted. "I prefer to not talk ill of the dead, but just for the record, he was a total asshole. Tried to screw us more than once. He's the one who led Spriggs, Low's compatriot, to the plantation and kidnapped Lisa. It was a pleasure—" He abruptly stopped talking.

"What? It was a pleasure, what?"

Jeremy took in a deep breath and exhaled. He glanced at Forrest and then back to the ocean ahead. "I'm the one who killed him."

Forrest fixated on Jeremy's eyes.

"He was about to attack Mason after Mason discovered his latest act of treachery. I hit him with a belaying pin, you know, to subdue him. Apparently, hit him too hard. He died a couple of days later. We were on the way back from that first trip to New York."

"You buried him on the plantation."

"Mason insisted. Said he was still one of the survivors and, in that regard, deserved to be buried on the property. Technically, he was a part owner. Personally, I'd have just dumped his body in the ocean and been done with it."

Forrest nodded his head up and down. "I guess you guys have been through a lot."

"Never seems to end," Jeremy said. "One thing after another. You have to wonder how any of us humans survived through the ages."

"You have a point. You ever think about why we ended up in this time? I mean, we could just have easily been hurled back to the time of the Neanderthal."

"Surprisingly, no, I never thought about that. I guess we're lucky, in a way."

"Hopefully, our luck will hold out," Forrest said, as he massaged the back of his neck. He stared at the pirate sloops ahead for a few moments, and then turned to Jeremy. "You did the right thing."

Jeremy cocked his head.

"About Nathan. I would have done the same." He clasped Jeremy on the shoulder before stepping off toward the bow.

"To answer your question—"

Forrest stopped and faced Jeremy.

"About what we're doing."

Forrest raised his chin.

"This is all we can do. We have to try. Mason would do the same for any of us."

◆◆◆

Sylvester stuck his head through the kitchen doorway opening. "We got injuns at the dock."

Karen and Lisa looked up from their slate boards, each having been instructing an individual student on mathematics.

The two little boys looked up at Sylvester as well.

Michael sat on the bare wood floor, playing with three small stones.

"Mato?" Karen asked.

"Don't think so," Sylvester replied.

Karen placed the slate on the bench, stood up, and walked to the open doorway. She saw two Indians walking toward the house.

Lisa joined her and Sylvester and the three of them met the two men halfway.

Karen recognized the smaller of the two as Yani, one of Mato's braves. The two of them were usually together on trips to Charlestown. She looked past the two braves, to their empty canoe tied up at the dock. Mato was nowhere in sight. She smiled. "Yani, welcome to you both. Is something wrong? Where's Mato?"

"Men hold him Charlestown," Yani said.

"Hold him, what do you mean?" Lisa asked.

"Say he steal blankets."

"Where is Mato right now?" Karen asked.

"Stone house near water," Yani said.

Lisa looked at Karen. "The watch house."

"Did Mato send you here?" Karen asked.

Yani nodded. "They say have trial, maybe hang Mato."

Karen turned to Lisa. "I need to go into town and find out what is going on with Mato and Mason."

"Go ahead," Lisa said. "I'll take care of things here. Don't worry about Michael."

Karen turned back to Yani. "Let me gather a few things." She glanced at the canoe. "Your canoe will hold three?"

"Yes," Yani said, as he stepped off toward the dock with the second brave following.

"You going to be okay alone with them?" Lisa asked. "Maybe you should take Sylvester."

Sylvester raised his chin slightly in agreement.

Karen shook her head. "I'll be alright," she said, as she guided Lisa toward the house. She glanced back at Sylvester. "I'll be alright."

Sylvester turned and began walking toward the dock.

"Maybe you should take the Glock," Lisa whispered.

Karen thought for a moment. "No, I'd rather you had it here, just in case. But I will take one of the flintlock pistols."

"And a knife," Lisa said.

"Okay, and a knife," Karen agreed.

Ten minutes later, with a knife strapped to her waist and a canvas satchel in her hand, Karen stepped aboard the canoe. Yani moved three bows, as many quivers of arrows, and several satchels to make room for her.

With the river's current, and both braves paddling, she stepped ashore at the Ashley River landing in just over an hour. With the two braves following, she marched into the watch house twenty minutes after that.

Just as reported, Mato occupied the holding cell. It was just Mato; there was no sign of Mason.

Mato got to his feet when Karen entered the doorway. His only reaction was to raise both eyebrows. Even incarcerated, and wearing practically nothing, he stood stately and proud. He wore a loincloth, moccasins, and a cloak of deer hide draped over his shoulders for warmth. His painted face, mostly black, and the crop of feathers atop his head, apparently denoted his position among the people in his village. The feathers in particular—their number, arrangement, length, and color—apparently all meant something. In Mato's case, they were mostly just black and gray.

Karen didn't understand their subtleties, but she had seen him only a couple of times without the feathers and paint. And she knew he was held in very high regard. His loss at the hands of a white man would stir a commotion, even among the friendly Catawba.

Karen gave a subtle nod in Mato's direction and continued to the center of the main room. She came to a stop before the small table, behind which a single watchman sat. She couldn't help but notice the brown stain on the tabletop. It looked fairly fresh.

At that moment, Loughton and two other men engaged in conversation, stepped from a small office at the back of the room. He abruptly stopped talking when his eyes caught sight of Karen. He turned his full attention to her.

"We're doing everything possible to locate Mason," he said, as he approached.

Worry spread across her face. "What do you mean, what happened?"

"You don't know?" He rubbed the back of his neck. "Of course you don't, how could you?" He motioned for her to follow him outside where the air was less rank. "What do you know?"

"I know you and Mason had some kind of deal to locate Ned Low. And it involved Mason befriending a man you were holding named Libby. Here in the watch house." She turned her head, scanning the room. "I don't see Mason, or anyone that might be named Libby.

That's all I know. Oh, and we're missing three other men from the plantation—Jeremy, Charlie, and Forrest."

"All true," Loughton said. "But our plan went somewhat awry."

Karen exhaled through her nose and she tightened her lips.

"Ned Low's men, maybe Ned Low himself, showed up in the middle of the night. They murdered my two watchmen and absconded with Libby and Mason. Jeremy left word he was in pursuit. That's all we know."

"So, you have no idea where Mason might be at this moment?"

"I don't know where anyone is at this moment. But we have four vessels out looking. Low would most likely have headed north."

"And Mason is with him?"

"That would be the best guess, given the situation. If they were going to kill him, they would have done it here."

Karen stared at the floor, placed one hand over her mouth, and shook her head. The vein in both temples pulsated as anger welled up inside. That anger wasn't directed at Loughton, or even Ned Low; it was directed at Mason, magnified by the fact that there was nothing she could do. She finally looked up at Loughton. "I'm sorry about your men."

Loughton tightened his lips and gave a subtle nod. "I'm sorry about Mason."

Karen rubbed her right temple with two fingers as she glanced back inside to the relatively dark interior. "The man you're holding in there, he's a good friend of ours. We would not have survived our arrival in this area without his help."

Loughton stared at the open doorway. "He stole two blankets from the Edwards trade tavern."

"That's ridiculous," Karen said. "Mato wouldn't steal anything. He comes here to trade his pelts. More likely, Edwards tried to cheat him."

"There will be a trial," Loughton said.

"Over two blankets. I'll pay for the blankets. Tell Edwards I'll pay double or triple."

Loughton stared at Karen's face for several moment. He slowly blinked as he exhaled.

"He's one of Mason's best friends," Karen said.

Loughton raised his chin. "Fine. You pay for the blankets; I'll drop the charges on your friend."

"Release him now," she demanded. "I'll go straight to the tavern and square everything. You have my word."

Loughton gave a single nod and stuck his head through the open doorway. "Release the Indian," he ordered. "He's free to go." He turned back to Karen. "Tell Edwards this is at my direction. Just pay for the blankets. No need to pay double or triple."

"Thank you," Karen said. "And what about Mason?"

"We're doing all we can at the moment. We just have to wait."

"I'll be checking in," she said, as she turned to Mato exiting the watch house.

"Of course, Misses Mason."

She gave a tight-lipped smile at Loughton and then motioned for Mato to join her. The two of them began walking toward the Edwards tavern, followed by the two braves.

"Where Mason?" Mato asked.

"I wish I knew."

CHAPTER 10

"We have sails, Ned," the lookout broadcasted from his perch above.

By this time, in the late afternoon, Low's ship, Fortune, had taken the lead ahead of Ranger. The two ships patrolled an area about ten miles off the coast, and a little north, of New York. Mason knew the area well.

"She's a brig," the lookout yelled.

Mason stared into the distance, as did every crew member.

Nearly everyone on deck had stopped what they were doing to set eyes on what would probably be their next conquest.

The ship was just barely visible from Mason's point of view. But he could see enough to tell it was a large, double-masted, square rigged vessel. The main difference between a brig and a brigantine was the rigging. Both were about the same size, but a brigantine carried a square- rigged foremast and a gaff rigged mainsail on the aft mast, with a square top sail. The brig was square rigged on both masts, with a spanker on the aft, main mast. What Mason was looking at was definitely a brig, which fit Libby's description of the treasure ship.

"Full sails, Mister Thomas," Low said, as he stood in the center of the deck. "Signal Ranger."

"Aye, Ned," Thomas said. He immediately gave the necessary orders to the crew.

As one of the crew, Mason scrambled forward to help add a third jib.

Others scurried about, preparing the guns for battle.

Several men hauled powder and shot up from below and portioned it out for each gun. Most of the crew members worked to load the cannons and roll the heavy guns out ready for action.

Just as Mason finished hoisting the extra jib, Thomas came to a stop next to him. "Gun three, port side. Do what McGregor tells you."

McGregor was a middle-aged man with a barrel chest. He wore baggy, black pants tucked into nearly knee-high leather boots, an ocean-blue shirt under a black, wool coat. A long feather protruded from his wide-brimmed hat, which he wore high on one side. His complexion was a bright red, partly from the sun, but mostly from his likely overindulgence in rum. His hair was long and stringy, and he was forever brushing the thin strands from his face.

"Pappy McGregor," the man exclaimed when Mason approached. He held a cannon ball in both hands, at his waist. "Who might you be?" He spoke with a heavy accent, even less understandable than modern day Scots. And he was much more jovial than Mason would have expected for a pirate.

"Mason. They call me Mason."

"Know what you're doing with this fine piece of artillery?"

"I do not," Mason said.

McGregor handed him the cannon ball. "Place this with the rest of them over there. When the shooting starts, keep the powder and balls coming. And keep your head down."

"I'll do that," Mason said, as he took the four-pound ball from McGregor. The knowledge that the ball he held might soon be flying through flesh and bone suddenly flashed through his mind. He scanned the deck and saw numerous other crew members scurrying about. Each was preparing for battle. They moved in an orderly, deliberate fashion, in stark contrast to Mason's building jitters. Mason had been through it before, but that didn't calm what he felt inside. And despite Mason's nerves and his reluctance to participate, he saw little choice. Any sign of weakness or unwillingness would certainly garner an immediate blade to the torso and a one-way trip overboard. Mason placed the ball where he was told.

Mason raised his eyes to the blue ensign waving from the top of the mast. The royal flag emblem occupied the top inner quarter. The British flag was a common ploy for pirates. It allowed their ships to draw close to their prey before hoisting the pirate captain's own flag. Mason well knew that, in Low's case, that flag was a skeleton on a black background. Its sudden appearance was supposed to send shock and fear through the merchant ship's captain and crew. If the merchantmen surrendered immediately, they were usually allowed to proceed unharmed, minus their cargo, of course. Making a run for it brought retribution when finally caught. In Low's case, from what Mason had seen and read, retribution depended more on his mood at the time. Mason swiveled his head to Low, standing at the helm. He appeared to be in good spirits this day. Hopefully, he would remain in that state.

"More iron, if you will, Mister Mason."

McGregor's words brought Mason out of his reverie. He stared at McGregor's face, trying to understand what he meant.

"Below, Mister Mason," McGregor said. "Bring up more balls from below."

Mason gave a slight raise of his chin and stepped off to the hatch leading to the cargo deck. Just like the main deck, the cargo deck buzzed with activity. Men ferried rifles, pistols, and cutlasses up the ladder. Other men shifted cargo about, giving better access to the store of cannon balls and powder. From a crate butted up against the aft bulkhead, Mason grabbed as many cannon balls as he could carry while being jostled by other men doing the same thing and the regular motion of the ship itself. He made his way back up the ladder and deposited the balls into a wood frame in the center of the deck, designed to keep the balls in one place against the constant roll of the ship.

"That's enough," McGregor said, as he handed Mason a pistol and a cutlass. "Keep them out of sight until we strike."

Mason stared at the pistol in one hand and the cutlass in the other. He thought of the Glock left behind at the plantation. With it now, he could probably wipe out the entire crew with just two magazines. But it wasn't a Glock he held in his hand. It was an ancient firearm, with a single shot. He shook his head as he stuck the pistol in his waistband. He shifted the sword to his dominant right hand and moved to the gunwale. He gazed at the square sails of the brig, still in the far distance, with its stern pointed at the two pirate sloops. Despite the Union jack waving above, the merchantman was running.

◆◆◆

After explaining the plan to locate Ned Low, Mason's abrupt departure, and Jeremy's pursuit, Karen glanced at Mato. She wasn't sure how much of it he really understood, since he didn't respond. He faced forward while keeping stride with Karen.

"What I do?" he finally asked.

"You mean, how can you help Mason?"

Mato gave a single, curt nod.

"There's nothing any of us can do. The provost marshal has ships out, but we have no idea where Low is. We don't even know which direction he went."

"I stay with you until Mason return," Mato said.

"Glad to have you, but first, we need to take care of Mister Edwards."

"I no steal blankets," Mato said.

"I know, so tell me what happened."

"We bring skins to trade. Plenty skins for five blankets and some tools. Edwards say yes to five blankets; he give only three blankets. We argue. I pick up two more blankets. Many white man want to fight."

"I get the idea," Karen said. "Please, when we get to the tavern, let me do the talking."

Mato's jaw tightened but he otherwise didn't respond.

Karen entered the tavern with Mato and the two braves trailing behind. She marched up to the counter and locked eyes with Edwards. Karen had actually never met Mister Edwards, but Mason had described him. The short, thin, clean shaven man behind the counter met the description. Plus, he was dressed like every other merchant in Charlestown, with a white linen shirt and colored waist coat, in this case, green.

"The provost marshal finally saw the error of your ways and ordered Mato's release. You owe him five blankets and the tools."

"Three blankets," Edwards said defiantly. "And who might you be?"

"Karen Mason," she said. "The Jackson plantation." Mentioning the plantation gave her instant credibility as a landowner, in her case, the wife of a friend of the landowner, but Edwards didn't need to know all that.

Edward's expression immediately softened a notch, but he remained steadfast. "Still three blankets," he said, as he glanced at Mato standing behind Karen.

"Here's what's going to happen if you persist," Karen said. "I'm going to open my own trade store on the edge of town." She motioned at Mato. "Mato here is going to tell all his friends to trade with me at my store, where they will get a fair deal. It's that, or five blankets."

"This is the town trading store. By direction of the governor, the natives must trade here."

"You mean Governor Nicholson. I had tea with the governor's wife just last week." Karen watched the muscles in Edwards' jaw flex as he stared into Karen's eyes.

Finally, he lifted five blankets, two axes, and two shovels from behind the counter and placed them on the well-worn oak countertop. "Take 'em and go."

Karen stepped back from the counter and motioned at Mato. She then spun on her heels and headed for the door.

Mato and the two braves retrieved the items and fell in behind Karen.

Mato glanced back over his shoulder and gave Edwards a hint of a smile. He caught up to Karen and began matching her stride. "What happen?"

"Sometimes you have to force people to do the right thing," Karen said, as she continued walking.

◆◆◆

By late afternoon, the two sloops had pulled to within three miles of the brig. It had to be obvious to the merchant captain that the sloops were something other than Royal armed vessels.

"Our colors, Mister Thomas, if you will," Low said. "Run 'em up."

Thomas gave the orders and two men lowered the ensign and raised the skeleton. Raising the pirate flag was a signal to the merchantman to heave to, or face the consequences.

The merchant captain apparently elected to take his chances. After all, the larger vessel was armed, but less armed than the two sloops combined. More importantly, the brig was nowhere near as agile. But still, anything could happen in combat.

Knowing what he knew about Ned Low, Mason would have made the same decision.

An hour later, the sloops had gained another mile on the brig but were still well out of cannon shot. Mason didn't know the range on a four-pound ball, but figured it couldn't be more than two thousand yards, a mile or so, depending on the powder charge.

As the minutes ticked by, Low kept his gaze on the horizon, probably trying to gauge how much time he had before dark. At the current rate, there was time to catch the brig.

Suddenly, the brig came about to the starboard. The maneuver brought its broadside guns to bear on the two approaching sloops, which closed rapidly.

Mason counted eight gun ports just as smoke billowed from every barrel. He heard the successive *booms* at about the same time he saw multiples splashes in the water to the left and right of Fortune. He instinctively ducked, even though he knew it would have been too late had one of those balls had his name on it. On all fours, he crawled to the mast for cover.

With little more than a nod from Low to the helmsman, the ship began veering to starboard.

Mason glanced back and saw that Ranger was veering in the opposite direction at the same time. This was obviously a common maneuver against an armed adversary, something Harris and Low had probably executed many times.

The gun crews on the brig let loose another volley. Of the eight rounds, six flew harmlessly through the rigging. But two found a mark. One crashed through the planking of the sloop's gunwale, between two gun emplacements; the other caught a crewman standing at the stern and divided his torso at the navel in a gush of blood and tissue. Both halves were lifted up and over the side.

McGregor and the other gunners were unfazed as they took aim.

At Low's direction, Thomas yelled *fire* and all six cannons spit forth flames and thick clouds of smoke. All but one cannonball slammed into the brig's hull and deck. Wood splintered along the entire length of the hull.

"The rigging," Thomas yelled. "Reload, and fire at will!"

Every crew member not manning a large gun was aiming and firing a musket.

The brig's crew was doing the same thing from their own deck.

Between cannon booms, Mason could hear musket balls thumping into wood, or whizzing through the air. Armed with only a pistol, Mason would not have been expected to return fire, since the range of his weapon was much shorter.

By this time, Ranger had maneuvered around and was raking the brig's stern with cannon and musket fire.

With only a swivel gun at the stern, the brig was not able to return fire.

Low's gun crews were able to get off two volleys to the brig's one. That more than made up the difference in firepower. Cannonballs slammed into the large ship's rigging. Many struck home and brought canvas, yards, and line to the deck. Despite the damage, the large ship was still able to maneuver, and it did so by coming about to port. This suddenly brought its port guns to bear on Ranger. As soon as they were aligned, the ship's gun crews unleashed a massive volley at the sloop.

The brig's turn, however, exposed its stern to Low's gunners. They fired at will, volley after volley, without fear of return fire.

The helmsman steered in a wide arc around to the brig's starboard, while the gunners continued to fire ball after ball into the ship's planking and rigging. More clumps of rigging and wood fell to the deck.

When the brig's starboard guns failed to return fire, Low directed his ship to draw closer, broadside to broadside.

"Prepare to board, mates," Thomas yelled.

As the two ships closed, men scurried about and massed along the port gunwale. Some men held iron grappling hooks attached to lengths of line. When the large ship was within range, these men gave the hooks a twirl or two and let them fly through the air until they clanged onto the brig's deck.

This is when Mason should have joined in, to help tug on the lines and, when secured, board the other ship, ready to kill and maim. But he didn't do that. There was no way he could participate in the carnage he knew was to come. He had an alternate plan. While most of the crew were boarding the other ship, Mason intended to take that opportunity to exact his own revenge.

CHAPTER 11

After heaving to and letting the sails go slack, Jeremy, Forrest, and Charlie gathered at the port gunwale to observe the battle raging in the far distance. From almost ten miles out, they could hear the boom of the cannons and see the flash of discharges in the subdued light of early evening.

"That ship is most likely out of New York," Charlie offered to no one in particular.

"Hard to tell from here," Jeremy said, "she's large."

"Merchantman, headed to Boston, maybe London," Forrest said.

Charlie shook his head. "We won't even know if Mason survives this battle."

"That's true," Jeremy said, "but we have to pursue until we know something for sure."

"Can we get closer?" Charlie asked.

"As long as it's light, we'll be seen for sure if we do," Forrest said.

"We hang back," Jeremy said. "Observe and wait, for now. That's all we can do. That's all Mason expects."

In the dimming light, the three men watched the light show on the horizon.

◆◆◆

With hull-to-hull contact with the brig, Low's crew rushed over the gunwales with whoops and hollers. Pistol shots rang out among the clang of metal against metal as the cutlass-wielding crews engaged.

Mason had only taken a few steps toward Low and Thomas at the helm, when both men suddenly sprang forth to join the melee. Mason altered his course to pursue Low, intending to stab or shoot him during the commotion. But such was not to be.

Mason didn't hear the particular shot that sent the lead ball toward him, and had no idea who had fired the shot, but he felt the impact for a split second before his world swirled in a sea of black dots on a field of gray. The sound of battle, suddenly muffled, was his last recognizable connection with the world before all went dark.

What seemed like seconds later, his senses began to return, beginning with the sound of the two ships rubbing against each other, screeching from wood against wood. The sounds of battle were no more, replaced with human voices, indecipherable at first. He recognized Low's voice an instant before he opened his eyes.

Apparently only minutes had passed. The two ships were still side-by-side, but most of Low's crew, and Low himself, were still on the brig.

He raised his hand to the source of his pain: his forehead, just below the hairline on the right side. He felt the warm, viscous wetness of his own blood. He stared at the red liquid on his fingertips. *Bleeding, but not dead,* was his first thought. His next thought was the massive headache throbbing at both temples. He was prone on the deck, apparently exactly where he had fallen. He felt the wound again and ran his fingertips over the contours of the broken skin. A glancing blow from a subsonic flying piece of lead. He was unbelievably lucky to not be dead.

He suddenly felt hands on his upper arm and then a piece of cloth being placed against his wound. He shifted his eyes, focused, and saw McGregor hovering over him.

"What happened?" Mason mumbled. He was aware that his words were slurred.

"It bounced off your head," McGregor said. "I had a feeling you were the hardheaded type."

"Much blood?"

"No, it's already stopped," McGregor said, "you'll live."

Mason moved his body, intent on sitting up, but relaxed back to his prone position when his surroundings began to swirl and the headache worsened.

"Take it easy, you're going to be dizzy for a while."

"What shall we do with him?" Mason heard in the background. It was Low's voice.

"Send him to the bottom, Ned," came an immediate response. Mason recognized Thomas' voice.

"What is happening?" Mason asked.

"Ned is meting out punishment to the brig's crew," he replied. "They tried to run. They should have heeded our colors."

Mason shifted his head slightly but, from his position, all he could see was the gunwale and the heads of several men above. They seemed to be surrounding something. "I need to sit up," he said, as he pushed with his elbow against the deck.

McGregor grasped Mason's shoulders with both hands and helped raise his torso. As Mason came up, McGregor pivoted his body around so he could rest his back against the frame of the pin rail.

The world swirled for several seconds but then slowly dissipated. From the new angle he could see the men standing on the brig's deck, and what they surrounded.

Ned Low stood above a man on his knees.

The man was looking up at Ned. The expression on his face was one of acceptance. He was likely about to die, and he knew it. Based on the clothes he wore,

Mason presumed it was the merchantman's captain on his knees. He watched as Low lifted the blade of his cutlass slowly and let it come to rest on the captain's right shoulder. The sharp edge faced up.

The captain closed his eyes and lifted his face toward the darkening sky. His lips tightened as he readied himself for the inevitable.

Low studied the man for several moments as men from both crews looked on.

Every one of them expected to see the captain dead at any moment. The captain's crew cowered and tried to look away, but the impending scene proved too much to ignore. Low's crewmen jeered, smirked, and some even laughed.

Mason focused on the sloop Ranger as it crept by fifty yards off the merchantman's bow. Harris was obviously ready to lend a hand if needed. Mason turned back to Low just in time to see his expression change.

At that moment, Low shifted the blade an inch or two toward the man's neck and with an upward flick of his wrist, separated the man's ear from his head. For a moment, nothing happened. The wound didn't bleed, and the captain didn't react. But then the opening turned a bright red as blood began seeping from the multitude of tiny vessels. Blood began to flow. It streamed down the man's jaw and onto his shoulder, where the stream divided. Half ran down his chest, and the other half down his back.

It must have been that moment when the man felt the pain. His face winced as he clapped his right hand over the spot where his ear used to reside. He brought it down, stared at the blood for a moment, and then returned his hand to cover the spot. The man glanced down and to his right.

From his angle, Mason couldn't see what caught the man's attention. But an image of a bloody ear lying on the deck entered Mason's mind. Surprisingly, the captain didn't scream out or even moan.

The man suddenly bent forward and disappeared from Mason's view.

"Hold him up," Low ordered. "Back to his knees."

Two of Low's men rushed forward. Each took an armpit and returned the captain to an upright position, and back into Mason's view.

Blood now covered the entire side of the man's face, neck, shoulder, and upper torso. His hand still covered the side of his head.

Low slowly brought the cutlass up again, repeating the same motions as before, except he now let the blade come to rest on the man's left shoulder, the side away from Mason's view.

The man stared up at Low. His eyes drooped. The man looked tired, and his face carried an expression that said to just get it over with.

But Low wasn't one to be hurried. He took his time, positioning and then repositioning the blade on the man's shoulder. He glanced up at his men, standing in a semicircle around the scene. He cocked his head slightly to one side, as if asking for their opinion.

Several men jeered and urged Low to continue.

Without any additional thought or a care in the world, he flicked the blade up.

Mason expected to see man's other ear fly up into the air and plop back to the deck. But it didn't.

The captain immediately brought his left hand up to cover the spot as he continued to eye Ned Low.

At that moment, Thomas hurried up to Low. "We found it. A large chest full of silver, too heavy for four men to carry."

"Transfer the silver, a bag at a time if you have to," Low said, as he glanced around at the open ocean. His eyes landed on Ranger for a few moments and then turned back to Thomas. "Get us moving, Mister Thomas."

"What of him?" Thomas asked, motioning to the captain. "And the others?"

"Bring 'em; sink their ship. It will send a message when they reach port. We'll hand them over to the next vessel we stop."

"Aye, Ned," Thomas said, as he turned and hurried off.

The captain, minus an ear, slowly brought his left hand down, expecting to see it covered with blood. His hand was clean. He felt the side of his head. His face relaxed, apparently relieved Low had taken only one of his ears.

Low stepped over the gunwale and back onto the deck of Fortune. He stopped next to Mason. "Will he live?" he asked McGregor.

"He'll live."

"Get him wrapped up and below. Give him a day of rest." With that, Low turned and began walking toward the aft hatch.

❖❖❖

Karen and Lisa sat across from each other at their table in the common dining area. They each had both hands wrapped around a mug of hot coffee.

All of the workers had already eaten and were off to their various tasks for the day. Only Marie and her young assistant remained, and they both busied themselves in the cooking area.

This was the part of the day when Karen and Lisa didn't have to worry about what Michael might be getting into. He would be asleep for at least another hour, upstairs in the main house.

"You look worried," Lisa finally said, to break the silence.

"Don't think this thing is going according to Mason's plan," Karen said.

"Things rarely do. But he always finds a way through it." She patted Karen on the hand. "And he will this time."

Karen cocked her head for a better view through the window on the opposite side of the room.

Lisa pivoted her body to see what had gotten Karen's attention.

They both watched as Mato and his two braves walked toward the kitchen from the work barn in the far distance.

Lisa swung back around to face Karen. "They could have stayed in the main house, we offered."

"I've lost count how many times Mato has visited and he's never wanted to sleep in the house, always the barn. Not even with Charlie, in Charlie's room. Every time, they spread out their bedrolls and sleep on the floor in the main section."

"Ever think about how this country has treated, is treating, the natives?"

"Yeah, all the time, but there's nothing we can do except our small part."

"They should have repelled Columbus before he ever stepped foot on this continent," Lisa said.

"I don't believe Columbus ever reached North America. The closest he came to the northern mainland was the Bahamas."

"You know what I mean," Lisa said.

"I do. But even if the natives had repelled Columbus wherever he landed, Europeans would have kept coming. They knew it was here. That's all it took. Besides, the Vikings and maybe even the Phoenicians and Romans were here before Columbus. And it's not like the various tribes were tolerant of each other before we arrived. They weren't. They're human; we don't play well with each other."

"Why is that?"

"Created this way. It's in our nature. But greed, envy, and aggression have their good points. It is those very characteristics that drive us to not only survive, but to flourish. Can you imagine beings as fragile as us, just surviving on this hostile planet for very long, much less achieving what we've achieved, even up to this point. Pure meanness, that's the only explanation."

"You've given this a lot of thought," Lisa said.

"Not really. It's something Mason talks about. He likes it when I listen to him; hates it when I don't." The corners of her eyes suddenly wrinkled and her lips tightened.

"He'll be back before you know it," Lisa comforted.

"Morning," Karen greeted Mato and his braves as they stepped through the kitchen doorway. They each carried a bow and a quiver of arrows.

"Morning," Mato said.

Yani and the other brave grunted something unintelligible.

Karen and Lisa smiled as Karen motioned for them to take a seat at the table.

The three men sat down, Mato next to Lisa, and the two braves next to Karen. They placed their bows and arrows on an adjacent table.

Karen had long gotten used to men, and women, who hadn't bathed in weeks or months. White people in this era were major offenders. Indians, on the other hand, were much more hygienic. They took baths nearly every day, no matter the time of year. And they often used various plant extracts for their skin and hair, giving both a mild aroma. And their teeth were generally in much better condition. In Karen's opinion, in the area of body care, the Indians were definitely the more civilized during this era.

Lisa got to her feet. "Let me get you gentlemen a bowl of our best porridge," she said, as she stepped off toward the cooking room and the large pot hanging in the hearth.

"Way Marie make," Yani said.

"Three bowls of oats, with cinnamon and molasses, coming up."

Karen turned her head to Mato. "I have no idea when Mason might be back. You're welcome, of course, to stay as long as you want, but it might be a while."

"We stay," Mato said.

Lisa returned carrying one bowl, with Marie trailing behind with two more. They sat the bowls in front of Mato and his braves, along with a pewter spoon each.

Maria smiled and then returned to her work area.

Yani wasted no time digging in.

"We hunt, fish today," Mato said, as he finished chewing a bite.

"Some fish would be nice for dinner," Karen said, as she stood up. "I need to check on Michael."

She was about to step through the open doorway when she came to an abrupt stop.

"What is it?" Lisa asked.

"Men coming up from the dock," Karen said. "Five of them. And they're armed with muskets." She spun back around to face Lisa, still sitting at the table. "Just to be safe, how about covering us from inside, if you know what I mean?"

Lisa nodded, got up, exited the kitchen, walked straight to the main house's back porch, and entered the back door.

"I'll find out what they want," Karen said, glancing back at Mato. "Finish your breakfast." Without giving Mato a chance to respond, she turned and headed through the doorway.

CHAPTER 12

Karen immediately identified two of the men. The one in front was Edwards, from the trading tavern. Just behind him walked his helper at the tavern, the Paul Bunyan lookalike that Mason had described. He stood at least a head above all the others. Karen didn't know the other three men by name, but had seen them around town. They generally did odd jobs.

"Mister Jackson or Mason about?" Edwards asked.

"What's this about?" Karen asked, as she came to a stop a few yards from the group.

The men stopped walking. All eyes were on Karen.

"I have business with either one of your menfolk. If not one of them, how about Charlie?" Edwards swiveled his head around to scan the area. "Charlie about?"

"They're expected back anytime," Karen said.

"Just what I thought," Edwards said, as he glanced back at his men.

Two of the men snickered. The expression on the other two remained neutral. That included Paul Bunyan. Actually, most people in town referred to him as Woody. Karen didn't know if that was his actual name or just a nickname referring to his stature. Or maybe some other part of him.

At this point, all the workers within view stopped what they were doing and watched. This included Sylvester. He began walking toward the group.

When he was within shouting distance, Edwards raised the barrel of his musket in Sylvester's direction. "Stop right there, old man. Just turn around and go back to what you were doing."

Sylvester stopped and looked at Karen.

Karen tightened her lips and raised her chin slightly toward Sylvester.

Sylvester slowly began backing away.

She turned back to Edwards. "What is the meaning of this?"

Edwards' attention was suddenly drawn to something behind Karen. She turned and saw Mato and his two braves step from the kitchen.

Edwards jabbed his musket's barrel in their direction. "If the men aren't around, my business is with them."

"They are my guests," Karen said defiantly. "Any business on this plantation is my business."

"Careful *you* don't become my business," Edwards said. He motioned toward Mato. "Take 'em."

Woody and the three other men raised their muskets and stepped off toward Mato and the braves.

They had only taken a few steps when all four stopped in unison.

Karen glanced back and saw that Mato and the braves had each drawn a knife.

"We no go with you," Mato said.

"Have it your way," Edwards said. "Shoot 'em."

Woody and the three men hesitated a split second before raising their rifles. One man fired just as Mato and the braves ducked back inside the kitchen. The ball splintered the wood door jam.

Karen caught movement in her periphery and glanced to see Lisa step to the porch. She held a flintlock pistol outstretched with a two-handed grip. She figured the Glock was just inside the door, and within arm's reach. She had the pistol trained on Edwards before the other men even noticed her standing there.

"Put the gun down, little lady," Edwards said. "No one needs to get hurt."

"You just tried to shoot my guests," Karen said, as she started backing away toward the porch.

Before Karen or Lisa could react, Edwards rushed forward and grabbed Karen around the waist with one arm. He pulled her close to his body as a shield against Lisa's pistol.

Karen's feet were free but missed the chance to stomp on his instep when he lifted her off the ground. She tried driving her elbows back, but it was like pounding an anvil with a marshmallow. It had zero effect. He was thin, but very strong.

Lisa pivoted and took aim at the four men closer to the kitchen. "Let her go or someone dies."

Keeping their eyes on Lisa, the four men stepped backwards in the direction of the dock, and the jolly boat tied up there.

Karen struggled against Edwards' arm. "Let me go," she screamed.

More and more workers stopped what they were doing and began walking toward the main house.

"We need to get out of here," Woody said loud enough for Edwards to hear.

As Woody and the other three stepped slowly past the back porch, Lisa cocked the pistol and aimed it at the nearest man.

"Karen, here, for the three braves," Edwards said, "then we'll be out of here."

Karen was well aware that Edwards had already gone past the point of letting this whole thing just pass. He had manhandled her, and his men had fired at Mato. Mason would not let that go. She was pretty sure Edwards knew that as well.

"You're only making things worse," Karen said. "Let me go, leave peacefully, and no harm will come to you."

"Harm come to me," Edwards said, "look around. Five armed men against a pistol."

As Edwards spoke, Karen caught movement out of the corner of her eye. Before the source could register, Karen heard a loud *whap* and Edwards' hold on her went instantly limp. As he crumpled, he dragged Karen with him, until they were both sprawled on the ground.

Looking up, she saw Mato standing above her, holding a length of oak limb in his hand.

Yani and the other brave stood just behind him. Each held a bow, with an arrow ready to release.

Woody and the three men, hearing the noise, spun around.

Facing the two bowmen and Lisa still aiming the pistol, the tension released from all four of their bodies.

"Where did you come from?" Woody asked.

"Back window," Mato said. "Take Edwards, leave."

Karen scrambled to her feet just as Lisa arrived at her side. "You heard him."

Two of the men grabbed Edwards by the armpits and dragged him toward the dock.

"He's not going to be happy about this," Woody said, as he turned back and faced Karen and the others.

"We won't be so pleasant next time," Lisa said. "And I suspect Mason and Jeremy won't be too happy about your visit. You may be getting a visit from them."

Woody tightened his lips, turned, and joined the others.

Karen watched as the four men loaded Edwards into the jolly boat, pushed off from the dock, and began the journey back to Charlestown.

Lisa turned to Mato. "Thank you."

"Yes, thank you, Mato," Karen said. "It could have turned out much differently had you not been here."

"They not come if I not here," Mato said.

"That won't matter to Mason and Jeremy," Karen said. "You are friends. We will help if we can, no matter the trouble."

"Finish porridge now," Yani said, as he started walking toward the kitchen.

◆◆◆

Mason was aware of sounds first. Men mumbled, wood knocked against wood, and the ship creaked from the strains of moving through the water under sail. He heard Low's voice from somewhere in the distance, yelling something he couldn't understand. Then he became aware of the throbbing in his head. He opened his eyes and tried to focus on the overhead, the wood planks of the deck above. In the dull light, the seams between the planks traveled before his eyes. He shifted his head and realized he was still in the hammock from the day before. The hammock swung gently in rhythm with the ship. That movement, as it turned out, accounted for the movement before his eyes. He tried to raise up, winced, and fell back. He felt the rough cloth of the bandage around his head.

He heard shuffling.

A man's voice barked from somewhere near. "How you feeling?" McGregor asked.

"Better than yesterday, I think. Still have the headache."

"Dizzy? Feel sick?"

"Hard to tell about the dizziness on this ship. Stomach feels well enough."

"Try getting to your feet," McGregor said. "Ned wants you on the cannon. Said to make you a first-rate gunner."

Mason swung his feet over the side and sat up. The room swirled a time or two but then normalized. Holding onto McGregor's shoulder with one hand, he rose to his feet. He stood there a moment. "I think I'm alright."

"Better than being dead," McGregor said. "Something to eat or drink?"

His choices were likely a brick-hard biscuit and ale or grog to wash it down. "Maybe later," he said, as he took a step. "Just need to walk around a bit."

"That's good," McGregor said. "Walk it off."

Mason smirked, wondering how far back in history that term went.

"All you need is a little rum," McGregor said, as he directed Mason to one of the crew tables forward, toward the galley.

Mason slid onto the bench and was about to object when McGregor slammed a pewter mug before him. Mason lifted the mug and took a whiff. "Got any water?"

"Sure," he said, as he stepped into the galley area and returned with a ladle filled to the brim. Some sloshed out from the movement of the ship. He poured the ladle into the mug with the rum.

Mason exhaled at the thought of drinking with a concussion. "Thank you," he said, as he picked up the mug. He took another whiff and then allowed a couple of sips to pass between his lips. He sat the mug back on the table. "Where we headed?"

McGregor straddled Mason's bench. "Given our profits from yesterday, hard to say. I heard Ned say something about maybe headin' south. The islands. Maybe cross over."

"Cross over?"

"Head east."

Europe, the Med, the Azores. That's exactly where Mason didn't want to go. He might never find his way back home.

"Surely there are lucrative targets to be had on this coast."

"I think Ned has worn out his welcome hereabouts," McGregor said. "But none of that matters to us. I just need to get you on them guns. We're short men."

Mason took another sip and placed the mug down. "Lead the way."

"Good man," McGregor said, as he slapped Mason on the back.

Mason followed McGregor up the ladder to the main deck and over to the gun McGregor had operated during the previous battle.

McGregor stopped next to the carriage and kicked the butt of the iron gun. "She's a minion, a four-pounder." He pointed to the deck next to the cannon, where several long poles with various tools mounted on the end of each were lying. "Pick up the worm there."

Mason wasn't sure which tool he referred to but guessed it was the pole with an iron corkscrew on one end. He picked up the tool.

"Used for removing debris from the breech after it's fired." He motioned Mason toward the end of the barrel. "Run it down and give it a twist."

As instructed, Mason inserted the worm end of the tool into the barrel, ran it to the breech, twisted clockwise, and pulled the tool from the barrel.

"Good, now the swab."

Mason eyed another long pole with a stained clump of sheepskin affixed to one end.

"Give it a quick dunk first."

Mason picked up the swab, dunked it into a pail of water, slung it through the air a couple of times to remove the excess, plunged it down the barrel and immediately back out.

"We're ready for the charge," McGregor said. "You'll need the ladle."

Mason picked up the third instrument, a long pole with a brass canister at one end, shaped like the tip of a giant hypodermic needle. Mason guessed the ladle was sized to deliver the exact amount of powder needed for a 4-pound ball.

"Fill it with powder from the satchel."

The satchel turned out to be a cylindrical container a little longer, but narrower, than a water pail.

Mason followed the instructions, filling the ladle with black powder, inserting the end into the barrel all the way down to the breech, and then twisting the pole to deposit the powder. He removed the ladle, laid it next to the other tools, and looked at McGregor for the next step.

Various crewmen, busy about the area, snickered from time to time, probably at the slow and methodical manner in which McGregor instructed.

"Don't worry about them, several have blown themselves up because they didn't listen." He nodded to a bin near the carriage, containing pieces of rag. "Wadding next. Use the ram to pack it tight."

Mason picked up the fourth and last of the tools, a long pole with a round, wood end, about the diameter of the cannon's barrel. He used it to push the wadding down the barrel, tamped it good, and removed the ram. He immediately picked up a 4-pound ball from the rack next to the carriage and turned to the gun.

"Another piece of wadding. Don't want the ball to roll out on you."

Mason grabbed another piece of wadding, let the ball roll down the barrel, and then followed it with the ram to send the last piece of wadding into position.

"She's loaded, now for the priming." McGregor handed Mason a powder horn and an icepick-looking tool. "Prick the vent and fill it with powder."

Mason used the icepick to clear the vent hole on the butt of the gun, and then filled the vent with powder.

"She's ready to fire," McGregor said. "Just need to roll her out and align the barrel." He bent down and picked up the free end of a line running from a block and tackle on one side. He motioned for Mason to pick up the opposite line. Together they pulled on the lines, which moved the carriage closer to the hull and protruded the barrel to port.

"Adjust the quoin," McGregor said.

"The what?"

McGregor pointed. "The wedge of wood under the butt, to raise and lower the barrel."

Mason pulled on the wedge until it slid back a couple of inches, which raised the barrel.

"That's good." He handed Mason a stick with a one-foot length of rope attached to one end. Smoke wafted from the end. "Blow on the slow match and strike the vent."

Mason blew on the end of the rope until the ember glowed bright red. He covered his near ear with one hand and touched the slow match to the vent. The powder in the vent fizzled, smoked, and the cannon roared with a loud *boom*. Smoke poured from the barrel and rolled across the water.

"Now, run through the whole thing again."

CHAPTER 13

"What are they shooting at?" Forrest asked. "I don't see anything except the tops of the two sloops."

"Impossible to tell from here," Charlie said, standing next to Forrest and Jeremy in the bow. "Could be something over the horizon, or nothing at all."

"Gunnery practice?" Jeremy asked. "Only one of the two ships is firing."

Charlie squinted. "Could be."

Jeremy turned and stepped off aft. "We have their course and speed." He motioned toward the coast with the flick of his left hand. "Cape Cod is over there."

"They could look for more targets around Boston," Forest said, "continue north to Nova Scotia, or—"

"Or head back to the Carolinas," Charlie said, cutting him off.

Forrest rubbed the back of his neck. "And if they reverse course?"

"We head for the coast until they pass," Charlie said.

"Sounds like a plan," Jeremy said in a raised voice from the tiller.

◆◆◆

"Set the t'gallants," Captain Solgard yelled. He leaned slightly to Lieutenant Smith, standing next to him. "Make your course south west, Mister Smith."

"Home, sir?"

"The man won't have gone farther north," Solgard said. "We head back, put into port for a night, and continue to the Carolinas."

"Aye, sir," Smith said. He stepped to the wheel and gave the helmsman the course. He returned to Solgard's side. "Perhaps there's news of his whereabouts?"

"That's what I'm hoping, Mister Smith," Solgard said, as he flicked a speck of dust from his otherwise spotless, navy-blue coat sleeve. He adjusted his cap, clasped his hands behind his back, and looked off into the distance. "That's what I'm hoping."

◆◆◆

Karen looked up from the slate at the movement in the corner of her eye. She smiled at the sight of nine-year-old Joe-Turner, shirtless, standing in the kitchen's open doorway. Her eyes immediately dropped to the dirty rag he held against his left hand with his right, and the growing red stain.

At that moment, Marie entered the dining area carrying an empty basket. She spotted Joe-Turner in the doorway and rushed toward him. "Lord, boy, what have you gone and done?"

"Sliced my hand with that old rice hook," Joe-Turner said.

"What were you doing with a hook, harvesting's been done for ages?" Marie asked.

"Gettin' some that marsh grass."

Karen got to her feet. "Here, let me look at it." She grasped Joe-Turner's wrist with one hand and the dirty rag with the other. She lifted the rag to expose the wound, but pressed it back when the flow of blood increased. "You definitely cut your finger." She grabbed Joe-Turner's right hand and placed it back on the wound. "Press it hard and hold it until I return." She guided him to the nearest bench and had him sit.

"What's going on?" Lisa asked, as she entered the room with young Michael in tow.

"This boy done gone and cut his finger clean off," Marie exclaimed.

"It's not that bad," Karen said, "but I need the med kit."

Lisa lifted Michael to the bench next to Joe-Turner and then hurried out.

"We'll need some soap and clean water," Karen said to Marie.

"Will he lose that finger?" Marie asked with a worried look.

"He'll be fine. But we need that soap and water. And a clean rag."

Marie tightened her jaw, took another look at Joe-Turner, and hurried off.

Lisa returned and plopped a medium sized black nylon, zippered bag on the tabletop near Joe-Turner.

With Joe-Turner facing away from the bag, Karen slid the zipper open. "Open one of the gauzes and we'll need the tape and a suture kit."

Lisa rummaged through the bag until she produced a thick gauze contained in a paper wrapper, and the suture kit. She quickly removed the paper wrapper, wadded it into a small ball, and tossed it back in the bag. "Sure you want to use the tape?"

Karen raised both eyebrows. "Maybe some strips of gauze or cloth would be better."

Lisa nodded and retrieved a second gauze package, which she opened and again tossed the wrapper back into the bag. She retrieved a pair of shiny medical scissors and quickly cut the second gauze into strips.

"And the ointment," Karen said.

Lisa rummaged in the bag, located the Neosporin ointment, but left it out of sight in the bag.

Marie returned with a bowl of water, a bar of soap, and a clean rag.

Karen removed the dirty rag from Joe-Turner's hand and examined the wound. The cut appeared deep, possibly to the bone. She had no idea if he had also cut one or more tendons, but there was nothing she could do if he had. The blood still flowed, but a little less than before. She quickly washed the wound with the soap and water and patted it dry with the clean rag. On the final pat, she held the towel in place. "Hold that," she said to Joe-Turner.

He held the rag with his free hand as he watched Karen work.

Karen opened the tiny suture kit, actually a practice kit available online, or at least it would be in three hundred years. She tore open the kit and unwound the blue, monofilament line already attached to the curved needle. She reached back inside the med kit and produced a small, plastic bottle of sterile saline solution and the instruments she would need for the sutures. She paused and looked at Joe-Turner. "This might sting a little, but it will heal much better. Can you stand a little pain?"

"Yes, ma'am," Joe-Turner said, as he vigorously nodded his head.

Karen removed the rag and quickly washed the wound with the saline solution under pressure from the squeeze bottle.

Joe-Turner winced and closed his eyes.

Karen continued with the solution for several seconds more, under as much pressure as the little bottle would manage. Finished with the solution, she stemmed the increasing blood flow with the gauze pad. "This is the part that might sting a little. You ready?"

Joe-Turner opened his eyes. "Yes, ma'am."

Marie, mesmerized by the process, stepped closer. "I ain't never saw no doctoring stuff like that. You squeezed that bottle and the water comes out."

"It's something new, Marie. We brought it from the far east. It will be in these parts soon."

That seemed to satisfy Marie, so Karen continued. She started by cleaning her fingers with an individual alcohol swab contained in a small foil pack. She next grasped the suture needle with a stainless-steel needle holder and picked up the tissue forceps with her other hand. She began about an eighth of an inch from the end of the cut and used the forceps to grasp the tissue on one side of the cut.

Joe-Turner winced again and closed his eyes even more tightly this time.

Karen had only practiced suturing a couple of times before she had to sew a deep cut on Mason, a year earlier. It turned out alright, and the wound healed without infection.

"This will sting, but it will be over soon."

Joe-Turner nodded but kept his eyes closed.

With the skin secured with the forceps, she inserted the needle, threaded the monofilament through the flap of skin, transferred the forceps to the opposite edge of the cut, and continued the needle and line. She pulled most of the line through, leaving only about three inches on the short end. She next took hold of the needle with her fingers, wrapped the thread around the needle holder three times, and then grasped the free end of the thread with the holder. She pulled the short end of the thread with the needle holder, and the long end with her fingers, until the thread came together into a knot, closing the wound's gaped edges together. She repeated the knotting process five more times, leaving the two edges of the cut pulled together with a tight knot. She then snipped both ends of the thread close to the knot. With Lisa dabbing the excess blood as Karen worked, Karen set eight more sutures, bringing the edges of the entire length of the cut together. Karen then poured a generous amount of Betadine from a small bottle over the wound and patted it dry with clean gauze.

She took another clean gauze from Lisa's hand, applied some ointment to it, and wrapped it around the now sutured wound several times, as tightly as possible. She used the cut strips to secure the gauze in place. Karen tugged on the strips tighter, wrapped them a couple of more times, and then tied them in knots. She twisted Joe-Turner's hand, examining the wrapped wound from all angles. "Done," she finally said, looking at Joe-Turner's still-closed eyes. "That didn't hurt that much, not for a big guy like you."

Joe-Turner slowly opened his eyes and looked down at the bandaged finger. He smiled. "It don't hurt none at all."

"I ain't never seen no doctoring like that," Marie said, as she examined and felt the bandage. "You done sewed the skin right back together. Magic, I tell you, pure magic." She stared at Karen with an expression of amazement.

"It's not magic," Lisa said. "It's just doctoring. It's something we learned in the far east. It's common practice there."

"Looked like magic to me," Marie said. "And you say his finger is good as new."

"No," Karen said. "It still has to heal. And he needs to keep it clean until it's healed. I'll need to take those threads out in a week or two. No getting that hand dirty until then." She looked at Joe-Turner. "You understand? No using that hand for two weeks. You come back to me if it starts to hurt."

"No working," Lisa said. "And we need to change that bandage in a couple of days."

"I will, Miss Lisa," Joe-Turner said.

Marie's smile stretched wide across her mouth. "Thank you, Miss Karen."

"He'll be fine," Karen said. "Let me know if it starts to look or smell bad."

Marie continued smiling as she took Joe-Turner by the shoulder and guided him into the cooking area.

"Will it be okay?" Lisa asked when Marie and Joe-Turner were out of earshot.

"If it gets infected, we have a remedy," Karen said.

"How much of the antibiotics do we have left?"

"About a third of what we started with. It has saved a lot of the workers from the fever."

"What happens when it's gone?"

"We're on our own," Karen said. She began gathering up the instruments. "We need to boil these and get it all back in order for the next emergency."

◆◆◆

"A ship," the lookout high above sang, "two points off our stern."

"What is she?" Low yelled.

"Small, single mast, gaff rigged," the lookout yelled back.

"Anything else in sight?"

"She's alone on the horizon, Ned," the lookout replied.

Mason meandered his way toward the helm, to within earshot of Low.

Low closed the hatch to his cabin and used it to step up to the fantail, which was only a couple of feet above the main deck.

Thomas followed him up.

"See anything?" Low asked Thomas as the two of them peered over the stern.

"Not from this angle." He cranked his neck up at the lookout. "Still there?"

"She dropped out of sight a few seconds, but she's back now," the lookout said.

"What do you think?" Thomas asked Low.

"Large enough for cargo?" Low yelled up at the lookout.

"Can't tell, too far to see. Single mast is all I have."

Low stared at Thomas for several long moments and then turned his attention to the horizon. He then pivoted and stepped down from the fantail. "Keep a sharp eye out up there," he yelled.

"Aye, Ned."

Low didn't know what that ship was, but Mason had a pretty good idea. A small sloop, single mast. Jeremy and Charlie. Keeping their distance. It had to be. Mason felt it. And for the first time, he didn't feel alone.

❖❖❖

"Shorten the sails, Master Scott," Lieutenant Smith yelled as the frigate came abreast of the Hook, the entrance to New York harbor. "Make way for the quay."

"Aye, Mister Smith. Dock her?"

"A good opportunity to hone your skills," Smith said.

Three hours later, after running a line out via jolly boat, the large ship was hauled into the wharves and tied up.

"Liberal shore time for the crew tonight, Mister Smith," Solgard said as he stepped from his cabin. "But have them back by morning. We have a very early tide. And top off our water."

"Aye, sir. Will you be bunking ashore?"

"Probably not, but I'll be late in returning."

"Very good, sir."

Solgard raised his cap slightly in salute as he stepped up to the gangway. Without further comment, he made his way to the dock and continued along the wharves in the late afternoon sun.

The Royal Navy had no base in New York, only a station ship which, at the moment, was at sea. Consequently, there was no Royal Navy office he could check in with for the latest information. That meant he would have to scour the taverns, and brothels if necessary, for any and all information available concerning pirate activity along the colonial coast, from Nova Scotia to Spanish Florida. The best place to find such information was among the merchant crewmen frequenting the establishments, and he would need to query them before they became inebriated beyond rational thought.

It was in his third tavern that he came upon a merchant captain with news of Ned Low. The merchantman spoke of Low's encounter with a brig, the loss of many of its crew members, and the captain's loss of his ear. The encounter had occurred only three days earlier, just north of New York harbor. A day after that, the captain and his crew were put aboard another of Low's conquests. That captain came ashore in Boston. But, most importantly, the captain reported that Low and his two sloops had continued north along the coast.

That gave Solgard at least a clue as to where to look. He and Low may well have passed in the night. Additionally, he now knew Low sailed with two sloops, making the man much easier to spot. By eleven that evening, Solgard had the information he needed to continue his pursuit.

◆◆◆

"That ship still back there?" Low yelled up to the lookout.

"Don't see it, Ned. Haven't for some time."

Low turned to Thomas. "Put out the lanterns. Don't want to lose Ranger in the night."

Night lanterns generally meant two for the stern, placed port and starboard, and one for the bow. That made it possible to tell whether a ship was coming or going in the dark.

Low watched as Thomas put out the whale oil lanterns himself. Shortly after, he spotted lanterns going up on Ranger, running several hundred yards behind Fortune. "Join me in the cabin when you're satisfied with the deck," he said to Thomas as he passed by his position.

Thomas raised his chin in acknowledgement.

Dinner in the captain's quarters consisted of relatively fresh bread, an assortment of cheeses, and a fine port taken from the brig, along with its silver. The rest of the crew could partake of the same thing if they wanted, but many opted for a hot stew of salt pork, carrots, potatoes, and onions taken from an island merchantman running rum to Boston. Much of the rum filled Fortune's stores, as well.

"Have you had a chance to count the silver?" Low asked Thomas, the only other person in the cabin.

"The chest is filled with individual pouches, each containing varying amounts destined for various people. I plan to count it all myself when I get the time."

"Set Knob to the task," Low said, as he chewed. "We've done well, but I think we should seek different hunting fields for a while. I sense we're being pursued."

"No doubt," Thomas said. "What of Spriggs?"

"Don't know, but we'll run into him eventually."

"Where did you have in mind?" Thomas asked.

"South to the islands or even farther south, to Brazil, east to the Med, maybe the Azores, or just lay low for a while. Maybe a final pass through the Carolinas before we decide."

"We're flush with coin and cargo, maybe a rest would do us good. The hull could use a good scraping. Nassau, maybe?"

"The Carolinas and then Nassau it is," Low said. He picked up his glass of port and leaned back. He held the glass in the air. "To rest and relaxation."

Thomas clinked his glass and they both drank.

CHAPTER 14

Karen was finding it more and more difficult to sleep. She went to bed early, hoping to wake with Mason and the others arriving at the dock, but then just tossed to all hours of the night. She slept little and usually woke well before the sun, and again tossed and turned. Such was the case this morning. She found it impossible to turn her mind off. Images of Mason being tortured and killed at the hands of Ned Low constantly flashed in her mind, despite attempts to think of something else, anything else. She couldn't imagine life in this place and time without him.

Giving up the pretense of sleep, she swung her feet to the floor and stood. She didn't know if it was hours or minutes before dawn, she just knew she couldn't lie in bed any longer. She slipped into a light robe, cinched the belt, and padded across the cold floor. She opened the door and stepped into the dark hallway. She immediately caught sight of a person's silhouette standing at the threshold of Michael's room. "Lisa?"

The silhouette shifted. "Couldn't sleep," Lisa whispered.

"I know just what you mean," Karen whispered back, as she stepped up next to Lisa. She peered through the doorway at the small form atop the bed in the nearly pitch-dark room.

"What if none of them come back?" Lisa asked. "Not sure I can do this without Jeremy."

The image of Edwards and his men appeared in Karen's mind. Without Mason and Jeremy, it would only be a matter of time before Edwards, or men like him, would show up. Lisa was right, without Mason and Jeremy, life would be intolerable. They would have to sell the plantation and move into town. A wave of guilt suddenly spread through her. After all they had been through, to just give up and walk away might be the logical thing to do, but it wouldn't be right. "They will be back, all of them. Have you ever known anyone with more will than Mason and Jeremy? And Charlie?"

"No, I haven't."

"There's no more sleep for me this night, feel like some coffee?"

Lisa stepped back from the opening and closed the door as she did. "I doubt Marie is up."

"I think we can manage a pot of coffee. If we can run this farm, we can make some coffee."

◆◆◆

"Enter," Solgard replied to the knock on his cabin door.

The door swung open and Smith stepped inside to the subdued light of early morning. "Just passing the hook, t'gallants set, and we're steering due east. What's your heading?"

Solgard looked up from the chart spread out on the table before him. "Anything on the horizon?"

"Merchantman arriving from London. Few fishermen about."

"The merchantman."

"Brigantine."

Solgard tightened his lips as he dropped his gaze back to the chart.

Smith ambled over to the table. "You were back late. Any news?"

"Word of an attack north of here a few days ago. Ned Low. Two sloops."

"That's excellent news, sir," Smith said. "That gives us an area and a target."

"It does, Mister Smith, but it's still a rather large ocean. And we're just one ship."

"I'm sure there are others out from Boston."

"No doubt."

Smith straightened up. "What are your orders, sir?"

"We're close hauled?"

"Yes, sir."

"Keep that heading," Solgard said.

Smith cocked his head but said nothing. When Solgard didn't look up from the chart, Smith turned and exited the cabin.

Solgard bent more at the waist and focused.

The chart depicted a rough outline of the colonial east coast, with not a lot of detail. Two sloops would be easy to miss on such a vast sea. Search farther out, or remain closer to the coast? North or south? He twisted the chart with his fingers until the coastline ran more vertical on the table. He twisted it back to its former position, stared a few moments, and then stood upright. He clasped his hands behind his back, paced the deck, and finally came to a stop facing the New York harbor, slipping away through the center window. The longer it took to find Ned Low, the more damage he could do. And it was only a matter of time before he decided to depart the area altogether.

◆◆◆

The very faint glow of the night lanterns in the distance ahead faded in the early morning light.

"We need to drop back," Jeremy said from the bow.

Charlie, manning the helm, pushed on the tiller, turning the boat a few points to port. "Zigzag or shorten the sail?"

"I think you've got the right idea, but keep them in sight."

"Why don't you catch a few winks," Charlie said. "Forrest will be up soon."

Jeremy's eyelids hung heavy. He closed his eyes for several moments, letting his chin drop to his chest. He looked back up, walked aft, ducked under the boom, and stopped next to Charlie. "It's either that or fall over soon."

"I'll keep a sharp eye, get some sleep."

Jeremy nodded, rubbed his face with one hand, and lowered himself to the bedroll tossed against the starboard gunwale. He had lost count of the number of days they had been at sea, stalking the two sloops. And he wasn't sure how much longer they could keep this up. They had started rationing food and water days earlier but eventually they would have to make land for provisioning. There wouldn't be time to enter a major port like New York or Boston. They'd lose Ned Low for sure. Perhaps they could make a quick stop along the coast, but where? They were sailing well north of the Carolina coastline they knew best. With his eyes closed, he rubbed his face again and took in a deep breath. All he knew at the moment was that he was too tired to think about it.

◆◆◆

Following a single rap on Solgard's cabin door came Smith's voice. "Better come see this, sir."

Solgard positioned his cap upon his head and opened the door. "What is it, Mister Smith?"

"Two ships on the horizon. Appear to both be sloops."

Solgard's expression brightened and his posture became even more upright. "From which direction?" he asked, as he stepped off toward the ladder.

"North, sir."

"Have you taken any action?" Solgard asked, as he took the ladder rungs two at a time.

"No, sir. We're still on an easterly heading."

"Good, Mister Smith. That's very good."

Solgard, with Smith close behind, emerged onto the quarter deck directly above the great cabin and Solgard's quarters. He scurried across the deck to the port gunwale and peered at the ocean. *Two ships, small, gaff rigged*. He nodded his head but said nothing as he continued to peer at the ships on a southern heading.

"Steer to intercept, sir?"

Solgard pivoted until he faced Smith directly. He stared at the man's face for several moments before speaking. "No, Mister Smith. We come about to a south heading."

"South, sir? What about the two sloops?"

He turned back to the horizon and studied the two ships for a full minute. He finally turned back to Smith. "Yes, Mister Smith. A south heading directly away from those two ships. Shorten the sails but keep the t'gallants."

"Shorten the sails, sir?"

"That's right, Mister Smith. Shorten the sails."

An understanding expression suddenly replaced the confusion on Smith's face. "You want those two ships to catch us."

"That's right, Mister Smith. But don't make it obvious."

Smith stared at the ships. "It will take hours."

"About four hours, I estimate."

Smith raised both eyebrows. "Very good, sir." Smith walked past the capstan, past the mainmast, and gazed over the open railing of the quarterdeck's forward edge. "Master Scott," he yelled.

"Aye, sir," came a voice from below.

"Shorten your mainsails by a quarter and leave them untrimmed, but only slightly."

"Untrimmed, sir?"

"That's right, Master Scott, slow us down a bit." Apparently satisfied that Scott had taken steps to carry out the orders, Smith returned to the helm just behind the mizzenmast. He motioned to the two ships in the far distance. "Steer to the south, Jonesey, away from those ships."

"Aye, sir," Jonesey said, as he turned the wheel.

The large ship slowly began to turn against the prevailing winds until its port finally came around to a beam reach. Normally, this would increase the speed of the ship, second only to a downwind with ship rigged sails. But in this case, the speed of the ship didn't change.

"Very good, Mister Smith," Solgard said.

"Beat to quarters, sir?"

"Not yet, Mister Smith. Let's see if they take the bait."

◆◆◆

Mason noticed that something in the distance had caught Low's and Thomas' attention. Mason stood up straight, turned forward, and gazed into the distance. It was a large three-masted ship coming out of New York. As Mason watched, the ship turned and began a run to the south, away from Fortune and Ranger. The British ensign waved from the stern. Had to be a merchantman, a big one. Its appearance would prove very enticing to Low.

"Trim the sails," Low yelled. "Make for that three-master."

"Are you finished dawdling?" McGregor asked, suddenly appearing next to Mason.

He motioned to the ship in the distance. "Going after the merchantman?"

"Of course, lad. That's why we're here. This will be your first battle, if they give us a fight. At least the first you'll be awake for. With two ships on her tail, the captain will likely give up."

"Where do you want me?" Mason asked.

"You can start hauling up shot and powder."

Mason nodded as he turned to the open hatch.

"Fill the rack," McGregor said. "All the racks."

Without pausing or looking back, Mason continued to the hatch and climbed down to the cargo deck.

Working as slow as possible, without being obvious, Mason began transferring powder and four-pound balls to the gun deck. At each gun emplacement, he racked the balls and secured a cylindrical, leather powder bag. The powder bags would need to be refilled during the battle since larger amounts of powder couldn't be kept on deck. As he worked, his mind was on the coming battle. An assigned gun captain at each emplacement did the aiming, so there would be no way for him to intentionally offset the aim. There was really nothing he could do to help shift the balance to the merchant ship. To even try would result in his immediate death. And him being dead wouldn't help the situation. All he could do was go along and keep his head down.

Mason kept an eye on the merchant ship as the distance between it and the sloops grew less and less. For some reason, they seemed to be gaining on the three-master quicker than Mason would have thought. Perhaps there was a problem with its rigging. Mason didn't know that much about ship-rigged, square sails, except that it took a large crew to operate them. And even with all the extra sail cloth, it was unlikely such a ship could outrun a lighter, sleeker sloop.

"Run up our bones," Low yelled from the stern.

McGregor scanned the deck until his eyes rested on Mason. "You heard the man, lower the ensign and raise our colors."

Mason was aware of a small, wooden locker at the stern, used to house the various flags, including signal flags. Walking past Low and Thomas, he joined a second crewman at the stern. The crewman began lowering the British ensign while Mason rummaged through the locker for Low's jolly roger—solid black with a white skeleton. He knew it well. He had seen it before on Low's schooner, when he attacked the airliner survivors on the original sloop. Mason couldn't have imagined he would one day touch that flag, but here he was.

He pulled the silky cloth from the locker hand over hand and let it bunch up against his chest. With both arms full of the material, he turned to the crewman just removing the ensign from the halyard.

The crewman bunched up the ensign and placed it in the flag locker. He took hold of the jolly roger's canton, attached it to the halyard, and then attached the lower corner. The crewman hoisted the halyard as Mason let the silk flow from his hands.

The giant, black and white jolly roger instantly began waving in the wind.

CHAPTER 15

"Beat to quarters, Mister Smith," Solgard said, "but keep it quiet."

"Run out the guns?"

"Not yet. Keep the ports closed until we come about."

"Aye, sir," Smith said as he hurried off.

Soon the sound of the rhythmic drums started up, quieter than normal, but very much distinct among the regular shipboard noises.

Solgard stepped to the front edge of the quarter deck and watched as the two marines, both dressed in bright red coats, played the familiar call to arms.

The crew suddenly came alive and began scurrying about the deck. The gun crews took their positions and began readying powder and six-pound balls. Other men poured from below. Each carried a musket, a pistol, or a cutlass. Some carried all three. The men positioned themselves about the gun deck.

"Keep yourselves low and out of sight," Solgard yelled.

Thomas suddenly appeared at Solgard's side. "Send the marines into the rigging, sir?"

"Not yet. Not quite yet. We don't want to give away our hand." Solgard stepped closer to the helmsman. "It is critical that you follow my orders quickly and efficiently," he said to Jonesey.

"Of course, sir."

Solgard gave a single nod as he turned his attention aft, at the approaching sloops.

◆◆◆

"Man the oars," Low yelled, as he gazed at the fluttering sails.

"We've lost our wind," Thomas said, standing next to Low.

"And so has the merchantman, but she has more sail out," Low said, as he stepped to the middle of the deck. "The oars, put your backs into it."

Various crew members began releasing the long oars that had been lashed to the gunwales.

Mason stepped to the nearest gunwale, pulled on the slipknot, and let several sets of oars clatter to the deck. He lifted one and placed it into the notch in the gunwale. With five crewmen ready on each side of the ship, Mason bent at the waist and began rowing in concert with the other men.

The ship immediately picked up speed.

Mason glanced over his shoulder at Ranger and noted that Harris had his oarsmen out as well. In fact, Ranger was gaining on Fortune.

"Steer to port of the merchantman," Low said to the helmsman, as he stepped to the starboard gunwale. He raised his arm in the air to get Harris' attention. When Harris stepped to the bow, Low motioned for him to take the merchantman's starboard side.

Harris gave an acknowledging wave and headed aft.

"Roll out the guns; our quarry isn't heaving to," Low said to Thomas. "Load, and prepare to fire."

"Aye, Ned," he said, as he stepped to the center of the deck. He began directing those not manning the oars to load the guns.

Every man on board was now engaged in preparation for the coming battle.

Mason stared at the merchantman, still in the distance but growing larger. They were gaining on her.

◆◆◆

"Full sails, Mister Smith," Solgard said.

"They're gaining on us sir, and we barely have enough wind to maneuver."

"Roll out all the cloth," Solgard said. "Let's see if we can squeeze another knot out of this breeze."

Smith disappeared down the ladder to the main deck and began directing men to the sails. He was back in five minutes to Solgard's side. "Looks like they intend to attack our flanks."

"That they do, Mister Smith," he said, as he continued to stare at the oncoming ships. "That they do."

Smith looked up at the sails. Some billowed briefly, some fluttered. "We just need a bit more wind."

"There's enough. And this way, we don't have to pretend to let them catch up." Solgard stepped to the forward edge of the quarterdeck. "Guns are ready?"

"Yes, sir. Just awaiting your orders."

"Very good," Solgard said, as he turned his face toward the sun. He closed his eyes and felt the warmth of the rays against his cheeks. He lifted his face for a better angle, to capture more rays against his skin. He visualized the coming battle, his maneuvers, and what he imagined would be Ned Low's response. He saw guns blazing, with smoke filling the air. He heard the clang of metal against metal, and the anguish of men. The acrid smell of burnt gunpowder filled his nostrils. There was no place in the entire world he would rather be standing than right here, planted upon this wooden deck, right now. There was no other foe he would rather be facing than the notorious Ned Low. The pirate. The scoundrel. His mind leapt in time. He saw himself standing on solid ground in the center of town. He faced a freshly built set of gallows. He watched the hangman's noose sway in the breeze. He saw Ned Low being positioned at the edge of the landing, and the hangman reaching out for the noose. He saw the light shove in the center of Low's back, him swinging out, and the rope stretching his neck. He felt the pats on his own back as men congratulated him for bringing Ned Low to justice. Come hell or high water, he would see it through, or die trying.

Smith's voice brought him from his reverie. "They're gaining; be on us soon."

Solgard opened his eyes and focused on the two sloops approaching from the rear. It was obvious they intended to trap the Greyhound by sliding up on either side, giving it no room to turn off or avoid the pounding from both ships. He judged the lead ship's distance at six hundred yards. The second ship maybe fifty yards more, and wide to starboard.

"Roll out the guns, sir?"

Solgard ignored the question as he continued to stare in silence at the approaching sloops.

"Sir? Captain Solgard?"

Solgard turned his eyes to Smith. The corners of his mouth raised into a subtle smile. "Patience, Mister Smith. All in good time." He turned his focus back to the lead sloop as he clasped his hands behind his back. That would be Ned Low in the lead ship. Low would need to be his initial target. He sauntered to the forward edge of the quarterdeck and gazed down upon the crew.

Nearly every face was turned up in his direction; each man waiting for the order sure to come.

Solgard saw fear etched on the face of some. But he saw confidence on the face of most. They were all good men. A solid, reliable crew. Solgard's lips tightened at the thought that some of them would die this day. But there was no better way to die than in battle for the King they served. They had fought together before. He had lost men. And just like those lost to the past, he would salute and honor those who died today. Perhaps he would be among them.

He gave a subtle nod to those peering up at him and then turned back and walked confidently to the helm. He saw that Master Scott had replaced Jonesey at the wheel. Jonesey stood at his side, as did Lieutenant Smith and one other of the ship's lieutenants. Solgard lifted his chin at Scott. "Hard about to port, Master Scott. Bring us along their port side." He turned his head to Smith. "Roll out your guns, Mister Smith," he said calmly. "Send your marines aloft and prepare to fire."

Scott spun the wheel. The large ship began its lumbering wide arc that would bring her guns to bear to port as they passed the lead sloop broadside to broadside.

"Make sure your gunners are ready, Mister Smith. They'll need to reload quickly."

Smith clambered down the ladder and stopped briefly at each gun position along the port side. He did the same along the starboard and then hurried back to the helm. "All ready, sir."

◆◆◆

"What are they doing?" Thomas asked, standing next to Low at the helm.

"This is no merchantman," Low shouted with annoyance.

"A ship of the line," Thomas said.

"Maybe not that, but a Royal Navy ship nonetheless. It's too late to turn off to port and we don't have the room against Ranger to turn off to starboard." The stress lines in his forehead suddenly relaxed as he stared at the large ship just completing its turn. "The captain waited until he knew we wouldn't have enough time to counter." He glanced at Thomas. "Don't just stand there, we're about to be fired upon. Let's get our shots off first."

As Thomas ran off, Low scanned the deck. His men were already scurrying about, putting their emphasis on the port guns. Low stared at the new man, Mason. He was following McGregor's orders, positioning munitions. There was something about the man, something familiar, but Low was sure they had never met. Low never forgot a face. Libby had vouched for him, and Low trusted Libby's judgement.

He faced the frigate approaching to port and then glanced at Ranger to starboard. Ranger would be blocked from firing. In fact, Ranger would be in jeopardy as the frigate swung around aft, behind Fortune, which it most assuredly would. Both sloops were faster than the frigate, but with this particular maneuver, their speed advantage had been negated. The captain knew what he was doing.

◆◆◆

"Fire," Solgard screamed from the quarter deck.

As each port gun came to bear on the sloop's broadside, the gun captain touched his slow match to the vent of his respective, precisely-aimed gun.

Each gun in succession *boomed*, emitting a large cloud of dark-gray smoke, and a bright-orange flame. Each carriage plowed back against its block and tackle, and each gun crew immediately got to work reloading.

Solgard watched the cannonballs slam into the sloop's hull or rigging in blasts of wood, splinters, and dust. He saw men go down, he saw limbs separated from bodies, and he saw blood. The Greyhound's barrage had taken out two of the sloop's six guns. He saw crew members immediately scramble to get the guns back in action.

Given the slight angle of attack, Greyhound's guns came to bear on the sloop well before the sloop's guns could acquire the frigate. All ten port guns had fired, and most had already been reloaded before the frigate moved into a firing angle.

The sloop's remaining four-pounders fired in rapid succession, and musket fire began raking the frigate's deck. Wood splintered but Greyhound lost none of its rigging and none of its crew.

At point-blank range, the marines stationed in the rigging, and along the deck, began firing just as all ten of the frigate's cannons *boomed* again with ear-splitting explosions of smoke and fire that swept the water between the two ships.

Again, the balls slammed into the sloop's hull and rigging, with devastating accuracy. Only one flew wide, just missing the smaller ship's stern.

"Mister Smith," Solgard yelled over the noise of battle.

"Sir?"

"Rake the stern with the back five guns. Save the front five for the stern of the second sloop."

"Yes, sir," Thomas screamed, as he dashed off.

The marines maintained a steady barrage as the cannon crews scrambled to reload.

Precisely as ordered, the front five guns held their fire as the frigate began making its turn behind the first sloop. The back five guns opened up mere seconds ahead of the front five. The spheres of iron tore into the sterns of both sloops in a mass of splintered wood.

"Get those port guns reloaded," Solgard yelled. "We need them now!"

Even with the confusion of battle, the acrid smell of gunpowder, and thick smoke filling the air, the well-trained gun crews didn't miss a beat as they immediately set to reloading.

By this time, the second sloop had started to come about in a wide arc to starboard. This would align its starboard guns on the frigate in a matter of minutes. The first sloop began turning out to port, away from the fight. In time, it would be able to reengage in coordination with the second sloop.

"Hard to port, Master Scott," Solgard said without taking his eyes off the second sloop. Turning into the sloop's arc would bring Greyhound's starboard guns to bear at about the same time the sloop could fire. "Mister Smith, tell your starboard gunners to aim for the mast, and for the port gunners to watch for the other ship. Your gunners may fire at will."

Smith hurried off, climbed down to the gun deck, and scurried from gun to gun.

The wind had picked up a knot or two, which aided the sloops more than it did the frigate. As a consequence, the sloop was able to complete the arc before Greyhound could get its starboard broadside around. Just as he was thinking the sloop would fire at any moment, all five of its starboard guns fired, almost in unison.

One of the balls flew high, straight through the rigging, but the remaining four plowed into the frigate's structure. As before, wood splintered and clouds of smoke rolled over the deck.

Two of Greyhound's crewmen were blasted off their feet. Another man, a marine dressed in red, fell from his perch high up, apparently having been hit with a musket ball. The man's body plopped to the deck with a dull *thud*. His musket clanged to the deck simultaneously next to him. He didn't stir.

A musket ball hit the wheel next to Solgard and tore a spindle from the casing. Well after the fact, both Solgard and Scott ducked in unison. Solgard raised an eyebrow at Scott as the two men rose back to their full height.

"Return fire, if you please, Mister Smith," Solgard yelled, without looking at the relative position of the two ships. Given their speed, he knew they were in position.

A quick succession of cannon blasts deafened Solgard's hearing even more than it already was. Several of the ten balls passed through the rigging, with barely a ruffle to the sloop's sails. A couple brought down lines and halyards. And then, after a delay of several seconds, Solgard heard a loud crack. He focused on the sloop just in time to see its single mast begin to fall, bringing the rat lines and rigging with it. The entire mass crashed to the deck with most of its length over the starboard side. The sloop came to an almost immediate stop in the water.

Solgard turned to Scott, "Bring us around her stern. We'll board her port side."

"Aye, sir."

Solgard rushed to the forward edge of the quarter deck and found Smith among the men. One of the sloop's shots had lifted a cannon and pushed it back from the open port. Its carriage rested upright, but off kilter. Smith was helping to lever it back into position. "We're boarding her port side, Mister Smith," he yelled. "Have your gunners fire at will until we're alongside. Have your port gun crews remain behind, in case the other sloop approaches."

"Aye, sir," Smith yelled back. "Prepare to board," he yelled, and then immediately turned to the port side to ensure those gunners remained at their stations.

Solgard returned to the helm.

"Perfect maneuver," Scott said. "Our guns will keep the other sloop at bay while we board."

Solgard gave a single nod and then turned to face the sloop. His eyes searched for the ship's captain, hopefully Ned Low, but it was impossible to pick out the man among the confusion on deck. *Just as well, they would meet soon enough, if he was still alive.*

CHAPTER 16

"The frigate is coming around," Thomas screamed from the bow. "They're going to board Ranger." He took off, running aft, leaping over bodies and debris. He slid to a stop next to Low, at the helm. "Why aren't we moving in?"

Low watched the frigate begin its wide turn around Ranger's bow, strafing the deck with cannon and musket fire along the way. He finally shook his head. "Can't approach Ranger's port with the mast in the water. And the captain of that frigate will stand ready to protect her open broadside. The frigate's cannons have greater range. And even if we could land a few shots, we'd be as likely to hit Ranger." He dropped his chin and took a deep breath. "There's nothing we can do."

"What do you mean?" Thomas screamed. His face turned crimson. Spittle oozed from the corner of his mouth as he spoke. "We have to help them." He spun around and focused on Ranger and the approaching frigate. He pivoted back to Low. "Together, we have her outgunned, Ned. Give the order to move in."

"We'll end up losing Fortune if I do that," he said sternly. "I'm not losing this ship."

Thomas fumed even more as he turned to the battle in the distance and back to Low. "Ned?"

Low shook his head, put his back to Thomas, and faced the man at the tiller. "Take us away from here. South."

Thomas' face turned even redder. The veins in his neck and temples bulged as he stared at the back of Low's head. His balled fists, knuckles pure white, remained at his side, despite his rage.

All of this played out within earshot of Mason as he and other crew members worked to clear the deck of debris.

◆◆◆

As Greyhound edged closer to the sloop's starboard, Solgard gazed at the second sloop, moving away in the distance.

"Perhaps we should pursue," Smith said.

The two men and Scott were alone on the quarterdeck as every other crewman gathered at the starboard gunwale, prepared to board the sloop.

"We'd never catch her," Solgard said. "Even in her weakened state." He turned to face the ship his men were about to board. He motioned with the flip of his hand. "We focus on the job at hand. Let's not get too confident, Mister Smith."

"Never, sir." He lifted his hat in salute to his captain.

Solgard stepped off toward the ladder. "Leave the port guns manned, with orders to fire on anything that approaches within range."

"Aye, sir," Smith said, as he fell in behind Solgard. He glanced back at Scott. "Take command of the gun crews once we're alongside. And you heard the captain's orders."

"Aye, sir," Scott replied.

◆◆◆

"What do we do?" Forrest asked, standing next to Charlie and Jeremy, at the tiller.

Forrest focused in the far-off distance, at the raging sea battle. The sound of cannon fire was distinct as dark clouds of smoke enveloped the two ships. The details of the battle were indistinguishable, given the smoke and distance, but it appeared the larger ship was moving in on one of the sloops.

"What if Mason is aboard that sloop?" Forrest asked.

Jeremy twisted his lips. He turned his head slightly to the second sloop, moving away to the south, currently two points off Jeremy's port bow and also in the far distance.

"That brings up an interesting dilemma," Charlie said.

Jeremy nodded as he glanced at Charlie. "Approach the battle or stay with the second sloop."

"Exactly." Charlie looked from the battle on the horizon to the second sloop, also on the horizon, but moving away.

"Fifty-fifty," Forrest said.

Jeremy exhaled deeply. "I hate those odds."

"Not really that difficult to decide," Charlie said.

Forest and Jeremy faced Charlie and waited for him to continue.

Charlie motioned with his chin toward the battle. "If he's on that ship, chances are he's already dead, or soon will be. If he does survive, he'll be arrested with the others and taken to—"

"Where would they take him?" Jeremy asked.

"From here—" Charlie scanned the ocean. "Probably Newport."

"To be hanged," Forrest said.

Charlie nodded. "Yeah, but there'd be a trial first. A short one."

"And Mason would have a chance to explain why he was on that ship."

Charlie pursed his lips as he gave a gentle nod.

Jeremy faced the second sloop, still moving off in the distance and almost over the horizon. "We follow the second sloop." He took hold of the tiller and pushed to the right while Charlie and Forrest hurried off to tend the sails.

The sloop began a gentle turn to port.

◆◆◆

When Greyhound's starboard hull was a few yards from the sloop, several crew members threw grappling hooks. Men heaved. When the two ships were only a yard from touching, Captain Solgard leapt from one gunwale to the other and down to the sloop's deck.

Nearly a hundred men, each armed with a cutlass and at least a pistol, followed and immediately began hacking at the opposing crew. Shots rang out and metal clanged against metal as men grunted and groaned.

Solgard sidestepped a toothless soul with a dagger in his hand and thrust his cutlass into the man's chest. The blade slid deep, neatly between the ribs, into the man's chest. As the man's knees buckled, Solgard withdrew the blade and immediately brought the sword up, over, and down on another man's neck. The man dropped to the deck and grasped his neck as blood began to spurt. With no other immediate threat, he took a moment to survey the melee. He quickly concluded his men would have the situation wrapped up in short order. He focused on the helm, in search of the captain.

Solgard had never seen Edward Low in person, but surviving merchantmen had. Low was usually described in his thirties, on the short side, stout, a little thick around the middle, both clean shaven and bearded. And one thing everyone seemed to agree on: he wore a perpetual grimace.

There were a couple of contenders in Solgard's field of vision, but neither were dressed anything like that of a ship's captain. For one, both men were barefooted and they wore tattered clothes. Solgard kept looking while he dispatched two other men, one with his sword and one with a pistol shot to the forehead. The latter man dropped in a heap at Solgard's feet. His head bounced against the deck and sent specks of blood across Solgard's tall, black boots.

And then, as if on cue, the sloop's crew surrendered. Swords, muskets, and pistols clattered to the deck. Hands went into the air. The battle was over and Solgard was victorious, with very few casualties.

Still pointing his second pistol and his cutlass at the sloop's remaining crew members, just over thirty men, Solgard stepped to the center of the deck. "Is the captain of this vessel still among the living?"

There was a long pause as the men of Fortune stared back at Solgard without comment. Finally, one of the men began getting to his feet. He stood up straight and locked his eyes on Solgard. "I'm Charles Harris, captain of the sloop Ranger."

Disappointment spread across Solgard's face. "Edward Low?" he asked, as he glanced at the sloop moving away in the distance.

The corners of Harris' mouth turned up slightly. "You missed him."

"We didn't miss you," Solgard said. He glanced at his own crew and the marines to either side of him and motioned to the Ranger's crew, all huddled together at the bow. "Put them to work cutting the mast away, but take it on board. Don't want to leave it in the water. We'll take this ship in tow."

Harris cleared his voice. "Mind if I ask where we're headed? And some of my men need attention."

"Newport," Solgard said. He turned to the closest marine at his side. "Fetch the surgeon and have him see to these men. But keep them under surveillance while they work, and shoot any man who steps out of order."

"Aye, sir," the marine replied. He climbed back over the gunwale and disappeared below the frigate's deck.

Solgard motioned to two other marines. "Bring Mister Harris to my quarters."

The two marines stepped forward.

Without being forced, Harris sauntered forward, stopping in front of Solgard. "You'll see to my men?"

"As long as they give us no trouble, they won't be harmed."

One of the marines gave Harris a light shove to the shoulder.

Harris began walking, escorted by the marines.

Solgard turned to Smith. "Take charge here. I want to be underway within the hour."

"Aye, sir."

Solgard fell in behind the marines.

Harris glanced over his shoulder as he stepped down to the frigate's deck. "Very nice of you to invite me for a glass of wine."

The marine gave him another shove. "Move it along."

"It's the least I can do, given your limited time left on this earth," Solgard responded. "I would say your days of marauding these shores is at an end."

One of the marines led the way to the captain's cabin, opened the door, and then pushed Harris inside. The second marine and Solgard followed.

"This will be fine, gentlemen," Solgard said. "Please take your station outside the door."

Both marines nodded without comment and took their position, closing the door behind them.

"Have a seat, Mister Harris," Solgard said, as he walked to a wood trunk and opened the lid. He produced a bottle of port and two glasses. He handed one of the glasses to Harris and motioned for him to take a seat in one of the straight-backed chairs at the dining table.

Solgard filled both glasses with the light brown liquid and took a seat opposite Harris. He slid a sheet of paper, an ink well, and quill closer. "Start talking, Mister Harris. Everything you and Edward Low have been up to over the last two years."

Harris took a sip and leaned back in his chair. He stared at Solgard for several moments before taking a deep breath and exhaling. "For the admiralty."

"Precisely, Mister Harris. And the court." He stared at Harris. "And posterity."

◆◆◆

Three men and Thomas sat isolated at one of the two galley tables, talking in low tones. They drank ale from pewter mugs. Other crew members were going about their business on the cargo deck, but none were within earshot of the four men.

Mason, returning cannon balls to storage on the cargo deck, took notice and began working his way closer to the men. Just as he got within earshot, all four men stopped talking and looked up at Mason.

"Can we help you, Mister Mason?" Thomas asked.

"Not particularly, just seeing to the munitions."

"See to the munitions somewhere else," one of the other three men muttered.

Mason didn't know the man's name, but knew him to be on the sour side most of the time and he seemed to be close friends with Thomas. Now that he thought of it, so were the other two men. Mason gave a nod and shuffled away aft.

Ever since they had left Ranger to the mercy of the frigate, everyone seemed to be in a particularly bad mood. The crew grumbled much more than normal.

Low had secluded himself in his cabin and had not been seen on deck since his decision to abandon Harris, twenty-four hours earlier. Something was brewing.

Mason climbed the ladder to the main deck and walked to the stern. He came to a stop next to the helmsman, alone at the tiller. "Other than south, where are we headed?"

"Nobody has said, but I suspect Nassau," the helmsman said. "Unless someone says different, that's where I'm headed. The night shift, too."

Once the man got started, his talking became non-stop. He seemed to have a lot to say, but none of it was of much substance. He talked about the weather, the condition of the water, what he ate the prior day, and other such nonsense.

Mason took the opportunity to gaze over the transom and scan the horizon. He hoped to see some indication of Jeremy trailing behind, but all he saw was empty water. If he witnessed the sea battle with the frigate, he might have elected to stay with Ranger, not knowing which ship Mason was on. As the helmsman carried on in the background, Mason contemplated his situation. He was in the middle of the ocean, on a pirate sloop, with a band of men without a leader. He dropped his chin and rubbed his forehead with his middle three fingers. He wondered how he could have ever thought this was a good idea. He glanced again at the horizon, hoping to see the tip of a sail. He saw nothing but water.

CHAPTER 17

Early the next morning, Mason was on deck, tending to the mainsail, when Low bolted from his cabin's hatch. His face was a ruddy red, his eyes bulged, and the veins in his neck and temples pulsated.

"Who took it?" he yelled.

Mason and the ten other crew members stopped what they were doing and stared at Low.

"Who took it?" he yelled again, as he scanned the faces of everyone on deck.

"Took what?" McGregor replied, as he fastened his breeches after having been urinating over the port bow. He began walking toward Low.

"The silver," Low said. "Someone has pilfered coins from the chest."

"How many coins?" McGregor asked, as he came to a stop next to Mason. They both stood about ten feet from Low.

"What's all the noise about?" Thomas asked, as he stepped up on the gun deck from below.

"One of these scoundrels has been in the silver," Low huffed. He pulled his cutlass from its scabbard. "And I intend to find out which one." He began walking from person to person, staring at each one's face for several moments.

"You haven't been out of your cabin for a full day," Thomas said, "how could anyone get to the silver chest?"

"Must've been before. Maybe during the battle." He stopped in front of Mason and peered into his eyes longer than any of the rest. He finally pursed his lips, shook his head, and moved to the next, which happened to be the man everyone called Knob, maybe because he was bald. And he was also the ship's quartermaster; the one who initially counted the silver soon after it was brought aboard from the brig.

"How do you know any of it is missing?" Thomas asked. "Did you count it?"

"No, I didn't count it, you wag," Low yelled. "But I know some of it's missing." He turned back to Knob. Low's face gradually turned beet red. Suddenly, he grabbed Knob by the scruff of the neck and pressed him down to his knees.

"I ain't taken no silver, Ned," Knob pleaded. "It weren't me."

Low put the tip of his cutlass to Knob's throat. "You took that silver. Admit it, or I'll run you through."

Thomas ran over and grabbed Low by the bicep of his sword arm. "We need to think about this, Ned. Need to be sure. If silver was taken, it's still on board."

With the entire crew now on deck, each man stared, mesmerized.

Even Mason, the newest member of the crew, knew Low could be totally irrational at times, and capable of unprovoked hostility. The man was insane. That was the only thing that could explain his extreme blood thirst.

With the tip of the sword still pressed against Knob's throat, Low continued to stare into Knob's eyes, seemingly oblivious to Thomas at his side.

"We search the ship, Ned," Thomas said. "We'll account for all the silver."

"Nah," Low gurgled. "It'll go over the side before it's found. And besides, Knob here sorted the coins. Probably took 'em then."

"I'm tellin' you, Ned," Knob pleaded, "I ain't got none of that silver."

McGregor stepped closer to Low and put a hand on his shoulder. "We can search the ship. There's no rush."

Mason saw Low's grip on Knob's neck relax just a bit as he continued to stare at the man.

A crewman stepped from the crew gathered around and thrust a mug toward Low's chest. "You need some rum, Ned. If someone took some of that silver, he'll pay. But we need to be sure." When Low ignored the mug, the man withdrew the offer.

McGregor let his fingers wrap over the front side of Low's shoulder and then gently pulled Low back.

Low released Knob's neck as he stood up straight. The deep lines in his face began to fade.

Knob fell back to the deck on his butt. With his hands on the deck to each side, he raised his torso a few inches. "I ain't got your silver, Ned. Like I been tellin' ya."

Thomas relaxed his grasp on Low's bicep. "We're all on edge about Ranger."

Suddenly, the lines returned to Low's face and his eyes narrow to slits. His jaw flexed. His shoulder's hardened. A millisecond later, Low thrust the sword's blade deep into Knob's chest.

The expression on Knob's face turned to disbelief as he looked down at the metal blade penetrating his chest. Blood began to ooze and run down his chest, bare where his stained shirt was open. He lowered his torso until he was flat on his back.

Low jerked the blade from Knob's chest and pointed it as he turned to the rest of the crew and pivoted in a slow arc. "This is what happens when you steal from Edward Low."

McGregor dropped to his knees and used Knob's shirt to try and stem the bleeding.

It was to no avail. Soon, the deck on both sides of Knob's chest was covered in his blood. Steam rose as its warmth mixed with the surrounding cooler air.

"I didn't take no silver," Knob mumbled, as his chin fell to one side and his eyes closed.

McGregor looked up at Low but said nothing.

Low returned the cutlass to its scabbard without wiping the blood, pivoted, and marched off toward the captain's cabin hatch. "Find my silver," he barked over his shoulder.

◆◆◆

Karen sat alone. Eyes closed. Dressed for the day in her usual petticoats, short gown, and shawl, she appeared calm and relaxed, as though meditating. Her arms rested to either side of a mug sitting on the rough-planked table before her. Steam wafted from the dark liquid, still filled almost to the brim. She licked her lips and opened her eyes at the sound of someone entering the common dining area.

"What are you doing?" Lisa asked, as she took a seat on the bench across from Karen.

"Thinking."

"About?"

Karen dipped her chin and pinched the bridge of her nose. She rubbed her forehead with a single swipe before raising her head in acknowledgement of Lisa's question. "Mason, Jeremy, Forrest, and Charlie."

"What about them?"

"It's entirely possible they won't return."

Lisa stared into Karen's eyes for several moments before she finally blinked. "We always knew that was possibility."

"In this world, in this time, it's more than a possibility," Karen said. "It's a likelihood."

"You underestimate our boys."

"Maybe, but I think we have to start thinking as though they won't be back. I've lost track of the days they've been gone. Is it days or weeks now?"

Lisa stared off at the plank floor, fixated on a smear of dirt. She closed her eyes in an attempt to hold back tears. But soon the water began to flow in a single stream down each cheek. She wiped both cheeks with the back of a hand. "I refuse to believe it," she said, as she looked up at Karen. "I'll never believe it."

Without her usual sympathy, she stared back at Lisa. "I've been thinking about Edwards."

"What about him?" Lisa asked, as she wiped at her cheeks again.

"He'll be back. I've run into that type before."

"What do you mean?"

"Twice. Stalked by men who wanted more than just a drink service."

"They followed you from the airport?"

"To my home," Karen said. "One of them did. He got in at night through a window."

"What happened?"

"I broke my favorite vase over his head and called the police. The other one just harassed me, mostly with phone calls."

"What happened to that one?"

"I was dating a first officer at the time. He paid the man a visit."

"And here we are," Lisa said, "no extra men around, and no police. We don't even have a vase."

"We have a Glock."

"To be used in dire emergencies," Lisa said. "Anyhow, what about Edwards?"

"I think we should take a more proactive stance."

"What do you mean?"

Karen twisted her lips as she stared off into space. "Something Mason always says. 'Don't let the battle come to you'."

"What does that mean?"

"Best defense is a strong offense sort of thing," Karen said.

"And how does that apply to the situation with Edwards? And besides, who says he'll be back?"

"He'll be back. I could see it in his eyes." Karen swept her hand in a wide arc. "Large plantation, no men except the workers, two young, attractive women alone. This is not the future. Societal forces are not in control of the day-to-day in this time and place."

"We have the means to defend ourselves."

Karen nodded. "If we know they're coming. We don't walk around with a pistol strapped to our hips." She paused several moments while she stared at Lisa. "I'd just feel better if we took the initiative. Take the fight to him, rather than waiting and worrying."

"You're starting to scare me, Karen. What exactly do you have in mind?"

"Go into town at night, wait for the right moment, and kill the son-of-a-bitch."

Lisa stared in disbelief for several long moments. She swallowed hard as she placed both hands on the table and leaned forward. "You can't be serious."

The somber expression on Karen's face didn't change.

"You are serious." Lisa looked around to make sure they were still alone. "You want us to go into town and kill Edwards?"

"Not us, just me. I need you to be here for Michael. Just in case."

"Just in case?"

"In case I end up on the losing end—"

"Or hanged," Lisa said. "One or the other is a likely outcome." She shook her head and glanced around the room again. "For one thing, how do you plan to get into town?"

"Mato and his canoe."

"So, you expect Mato to help you?"

"No. He'll wait for me at the landing. If I'm not back by a certain time, he'll return here and let you know."

"And what do I do?"

"Look, I know this sounds stupid. But I've given it a lot of thought. I'm not going to wait around for Edwards to show up when it's convenient for him. He made the first move. He put his hands on me. I'm not going to give him the chance to do worse." She paused, staring at Lisa. "You remember what happened when Nathan showed up with Spriggs and his men. We had no warning and no chance. They took you and there was nothing I could do to stop it. It's not going to happen again."

"Why don't we wait a few days? The boys will show up. They will."

"The only way I'm calling this off is if they show up today. I've already talked to Mato. He understands. And he's agreed to take me into town tonight."

"Tonight," Lisa exclaimed. "When did you talk to him?"

"Yesterday."

"Your serious about this? Tonight?"

"Tonight," Karen said with determination.

◆◆◆

Forrest covered a yawn with the back of his hand as he glanced back from the bow at Jeremy's approach.

"They just put the lanterns out," Forrest said, as Jeremy stopped beside him. "You sleep alright?"

"Yeah, well, no. Couldn't really sleep at all."

"It is starting to wear on a fellow. Worried about Mason or the girls?"

"Both. We don't even know if Mason is on that ship. And Karen, Lisa, and Michael have been alone all this time. They're bound to be wondering if we're ever coming back."

"Are we?"

Jeremy let out a long exhale. He shook his head. "What would you do?"

"Something I've come to realize," Forrest said, "not every problem has a good solution. Sometimes you're screwed, no matter what you do."

"This seems to be one of those situations," Jeremy said.

"Look, do you have any reason to believe the girls might be in trouble?"

"No."

"Then it seems to me, the problem needing a solution is here."

Jeremy gazed at the horizon, at the tip of a mast and sail just barely visible.

"For the short time I was around Karen and Lisa, they seemed like very capable women."

"They are." Jeremy put his hand on Forrest's shoulder. "Get some sleep. You have the tiller in about four hours."

"By the way," Forrest said, as he started walking, "we're nearly out of food and water."

CHAPTER 18

The hatch to the captain's cabin slammed open and Low emerged in a huff. He turned to Thomas at the tiller. "We still on course to Nassau?"

"We are," Thomas replied.

Low scanned the water, noting the position of the rising sun. "Why are we on a west sa' west heading?"

"I thought we would hug La Florida."

"You thought? You don't have the authority to think on this vessel. Only I have that authority."

Several crew members on deck made furtive glances in the direction of the conversation.

"Whatever you say, Ned."

As the two men continued bantering back and forth, Mason back-stepped a few paces to where McGregor was standing. "Why is he acting this way?"

"Harris," McGregor said simply.

Mason cocked his head.

"They were close friends. But even closer friends were Harris and Spriggs."

"Where is Spriggs?"

"Likely in Nassau this time of year, aboard Fancy."

"The schooner."

"That's right, the schooner," McGregor said with a hint of irritation.

"So, Ned will have to explain to Spriggs why he abandoned Harris?"

McGregor nodded. "And Spriggs won't be happy. That's why Ned is acting this way."

"How much more will the crew endure?"

McGregor's jaw tightened as he continued to stare at Low and Thomas, without further comment.

Mason, sensing McGregor was through talking, walked to the bow where three men were talking quietly among themselves.

They stopped talking when Mason arrived.

"How much longer is this going to continue?" Mason asked.

The three men looked at each other. Two of them moved off in different directions. The third man started off as well, but paused next to Mason. "Not much longer," he whispered.

❖❖❖

At dusk, Karen exited the back door and paused on the porch to scan the dock and river. She was dressed in a pair of Mason's dark pants, cinched tight around the waist with his leather belt, and an equally dark pullover shirt. She had her black hair pushed up under one of his hats, a wide brim he usually wore when working around the plantation.

Lisa stepped from the house behind her. "You sure you want to do this?"

"Deal with him now or deal with him later," Karen said. "I prefer to deal with him on my terms."

"That's all you're taking?" Lisa asked, as she motioned with her hand at the knife strapped to her hip.

Karen raised the satchel she carried in her left hand. "And a pistol. I hopefully won't need the pistol."

"Have you thought this through?" Lisa asked. "Do you know how you're going to do it?"

Karen wagged her head back and forth. "To a point. Play it by ear after that." She put a hand on Lisa's shoulder. "Don't worry. If it looks too dangerous, I'll abort."

"I suppose that should make me feel better, but it doesn't."

"Mato's braves will be here. And watch after Michael; he gets into everything these days."

"I know, and I will, but I really wish you would change your mind about this."

Karen smiled. "It'll all work out," she said, as she pivoted and stepped down from the porch. She began walking after a single glance over her shoulder.

Ahead, in the dimming light, Mato stood at the dock with his braves. "They will look after Lisa and Michael," Mato said when Karen was in earshot. He gave each of his men a glance.

They nodded without comment and started off toward the house.

"Thank you, Mato. We should get moving."

Mato held the canoe as Karen stepped in. She took a seat in front.

He stepped into the rear and immediately pushed off from the dock with the end of the paddle.

The water swirled around each paddle stroke as he pulled. Once the canoe was in the current, he used the paddle mainly to keep the canoe headed in the right direction.

Two hours later, in the pitch dark, the canoe slid up on the sand at the Ansley River landing.

Mato jumped out, getting his moccasins wet, and pulled the canoe completely up onto dry land. He did a three-sixty and scanned the area.

"There shouldn't be anyone here this time of night," Karen said. "The attendant leaves at dark."

Mato said nothing as he helped Karen from the canoe.

Carrying her satchel, she walked beside Mato in the direction of town.

A flickering torch at the town's west gate came into view first, a tiny speck of light in the distance. It grew in intensity as they neared until, finally, its glow bathed the entire entrance in a reddish gold dance of light and shadows. A single man stood guard at the entrance. A musket leaned against the wood frame of the gate.

Karen and Mato had already decided that Mato would do the talking. It would seem odd for a white woman to be out this time of night with a native. Karen didn't want to give anyone a reason to recognize or remember her. And they also agreed that neither Edwards, nor his tavern, would be mentioned.

She lowered her head so the brim would cover most of her face as they stepped into the light.

"Evening," the guard said.

"Just pass through to wharfs," Mato said.

The man stepped to the side to give them room.

Without further conversation, Karen and Mato entered the town.

Karen had been in town at night on only a few occasions, mostly for dinner or an evening visit with friends, usually the Trott's or Rhett's or both. Lit only with torches and lanterns, the mostly mud streets and grimy building fronts seemed less grungy at night. The dirt and grime wasn't as evident. But night brought out the rowdiness of the place. The laughter and jovial voices from the several taverns could be heard, even from the edge of town. The streets were crowded, and would be until all hours, with most people growing more intoxicated as the evening wore on. This was good. People would be focused on their drinking and carousing and hopefully wouldn't notice one or two extra people ambling down the middle of the street, as far away from the lights as possible.

Well past the west gate Karen came to a stop. "This is where you get off," she whispered.

Mato looked at her with a quizzical expression.

"You wait around here, Mato. This is something I have to do alone. We talked about this."

"I come with you," he said.

Karen shook her head. "Not part of the agreement. You paddle the canoe; I take care of business."

"I help you take care of business."

"No. You wait here. I insist. Otherwise, we just return to the plantation." Even in the subdued light, Karen could see Mato's eyes narrow as he studied her face. He wasn't sure what to do.

"Mason want me to help. Make sure you no get into trouble."

"This doesn't involve you or Mason. This is something I have to do." When that didn't persuade him, Karen turned to face him directly. "If I see any trouble, I'll stop. I won't do anything."

Mato's expression softened as he focused on the street ahead, in deep thought. "I wait here one hour. Then come find you."

"That's fine. This may end up as a reconnoitering operation anyhow."

Mato raised an eyebrow.

"I'll be back soon," she said. She took a final look at Mato's face, to judge whether he would remain behind. Satisfied he would, she turned and walked away, leaving Mato standing in the street.

She kept her head down as she walked, passing through areas without light to those of flickering flames. Her destination was the extreme northeast part of town. The Edwards tavern was on a narrow alley. She had been inside just the one time before, during the day, and had walked by it a couple of times. At night, it was darker than most, with its low roof and only the front door for light during the day. But it, too, would be crowded with patrons.

The town got relatively quieter as she passed through the middle of Broad Street and headed north along Bay Street, along the Cooper River. Most of the earthen fortifications around the edge of town had largely been removed, but the mostly red-brick wall along the Cooper River was still there. Karen knew that it, too, would eventually be removed. But, for now, it ran nearly the entire length of Bay Street, with several openings for access to the wharfs.

She passed numerous people along the way. Mostly men, walking together in small groups, laughing and hollering, already well on their way to total intoxication. Had she been dressed in her normal petticoats, she would have stood out like a sore thumb and most of these men she now passed would have stopped to solicit her favor. But, dressed as she was, they just passed by without giving her much notice.

Even in the darkness of the shadows, she dipped the brim of her hat at anyone's approach, kept to the least occupied side of the street, and kept a steady pace.

As soon as she made the turn inland onto Edward's alley, the tavern became obvious. It was the only dwelling lit on the alley. And there was a crowd of men bunched at its front entrance and into the street. Apparently, this was one of the more popular drinking establishments. As she drew nearer, she realized why. It was one of only two or three taverns where women of the night exercised their trade.

Several women laughed and cajoled, in an effort to entice the men to spend their money on something other than drinking. It was working on at least two of them. Karen watched two couples walking off into the dark, each wrapped in the other's arms. No baths in months for either of them, probably. Karen couldn't imagine the stench of the two as they wallowed in coitus. She shook her head at the thought.

She probably should have waited until later in the night for this endeavor, but she was here now, and she remained determined. The least she could do was make the most of the opportunity to gather intelligence. For one, she didn't know if Edwards lived at the tavern or elsewhere. She hoped it was the latter, since she would much rather confront him on the street. For another, she didn't know how long these crowds of people would persist into the night. She accepted that this would likely not be the night to fulfill her mission but, despite Mato's promise to come find her after an hour, she decided to settle in, observe, and gather information.

She scanned up and down the alley until her eyes found a spot that might be right for observation: a dilapidated building thirty yards farther down the alley, past the tavern. The small space between it and an adjacent building, just large enough for one person to stand, would be a perfect spot. She moved to the far side of the street and kept her head down as she meandered past the tavern. When she was sure no one was paying her any attention, she darted into the dark space she hoped was devoid of snakes and spiders. She leaned against the side of the building, just back from the front, and well covered in shadow. She folded her arms over her chest and watched.

In the early morning hours, the crowd started to dissipate. Several people had to be helped down the alley by one or two of their friends.

Karen had no idea of the time, but estimated it had to be two or three. She wondered about Mato. She expected to see him come lurking down the alley at some point, but, if he did, she never saw him.

An hour later, the tavern was mostly vacant, from what she could tell. Light from a couple of lanterns still flickered inside, but she saw no patrons. She rubbed the tiredness from her eyes and perked up in anticipation of seeing the man she'd come to confront.

A few minutes later, Edwards and Woody stepped from the entrance. They said a few words to each other and then parted. Woody began walking down the alley, away from Karen, toward Bay Street; Edwards walked back inside the tavern.

Now was the moment of truth. Confront him, or not? She had come all this way and waited all this time to do what, go home? She visualized Edwards and his thugs showing up again at the plantation. Only his next foray would be better organized and timed, perhaps he would bring more men. She had no intention of becoming a victim. *Take the fight to the enemy.*

Karen tightened her jaw and stepped from the shadows with the satchel in her hand. She looked up and down the street and saw only darkness.

The flickering from the tavern doorway was the only light in the alley.

She opened the satchel, withdrew the pistol, and let the satchel drop to the alley's dirt surface with a subdued *thump*. She took several deep breaths, in an attempt to get her jitters under control. It didn't work. Her stomach continued its summersaults, while the rest of her trembled. She nearly convulsed when Edwards suddenly appeared in the tavern's entranceway.

CHAPTER 19

"Who goes there?" Edwards asked, as he took a step closer.

Karen didn't respond and she didn't raise the brim of her hat.

"I said, who goes there?" His voice was deeper, more intent. He took another step closer. "We're closed, if that's what you're after," he grumbled.

Karen raised the pistol and the brim of her hat at the same time. She pointed the barrel directly at Edwards' chest.

Edwards smirked and grunted. "You intend to rob me, you scrawny excuse for a man." He cocked his head slightly as he focused on Karen's face. "You're not a man," he finally said. "It's you." He looked up and down the alley. With no one about, he turned his attention back to Karen. "You alone? You come to, what, kill me?" His gaze turned down to the pistol in Karen's hand. "You probably can't hit me with that. And if you do, it won't stop me."

That's something Karen had not considered. Unless she hit him in the heart or brain, the single musket ball probably wouldn't kill him. It probably wouldn't even stop him, like he said. The pistol began to shake in her hand. She reached up with her free hand and assumed a two-handed grip. "I guess we'll have to find out," she said, with a hint of nervousness in her voice.

"What's this all about? My friendly visit to your plantation?"

"Didn't seem all that friendly to me. Had it not been for my friend—"

"That reminds me," he said, "I'll be dealing with your friend as soon as I'm finished with you." He took a step closer.

Karen cocked the hammer and steadied her hold on the pistol.

The smile faded from Edwards' face. He looked up and down the alley again, and then back to Karen. "Even if you manage to kill me, you won't get away with it. I have plenty of friends. They'll figure it out eventually."

"Maybe, maybe not. But I'm not going to wait around for you to show up again, unannounced."

"So, that's what you're afraid of, that I'll show up again. How about if we come to an understanding right now. You turn around and go home, and I'll keep my distance. Sound fair enough?"

"Your word is worthless, Edwards. You put your hands on me once, I'll not wait around for it to happen again."

Edwards took another step closer. "We can work this out; don't have to be any bloodshed." Only about four feet separated Edwards from the barrel of Karen's pistol.

In her mind, it was now or never. She rubbed the cold metal of the trigger with her finger. *Pull the trigger, dammit.* She knew she had to, but she couldn't pull the trigger. Not in cold blood. Plus, she didn't want to attract attention with a gunshot. The night watchmen were sure to show up at the sound.

In that moment of hesitation, Edwards lunged forward and wrapped his large hand around the pistol's barrel. He ripped it from Karen's hand, without it discharging. He then stood tall and gazed at her as a wide smile spread across his face.

Just as she turned to run, his free right hand sprang in a flash and grabbed her by the shoulder, stopping her in her tracks. He jerked her back toward him while spinning her around. With the one arm, he pulled her tight against himself, her back against his chest and her butt against his pelvis. He tossed the pistol to the ground and wrapped his other arm around and grasped her breast. "Now we can get to know each other a little better."

As Karen struggled against his grasp, he lifted her off the ground, checked the alley in both directions, and carried her through the tavern entrance, closing the tavern door behind him with his foot.

"Let me go," she screamed, as she jerked her head in all directions. The tavern was completely empty, except for Edwards and Karen. "If I don't kill you, Mason will. People know I came here tonight."

"You already tried to kill me and failed. And as for coming here, I'll tell them I never saw you. Nobody can prove nothing."

Karen kicked her feet, squirmed, and moaned, trying to break free of his grasp. But his arms squeezed her like a vise as he continued across the floor, through the back area where he stored his trading inventory, and into a small room off to the side.

The room was pitch dark, at first. But then her eyes began to adjust to the small bit of lantern light filtering in from the bar area.

A bunk with a flatten, probably straw, mattress occupied one wall. A small chest of drawers and a straight back chair occupied the opposite wall. The room reeked of body odor and urine, just like the man himself. The only odor worse was the man's breath of stale rum and whatever putrid thing he had last eaten.

Her stomach turned nauseous and her face became clammy. In a time and place with a million ways to die, being raped and murdered was her greatest fear. She loathed the man holding her but, even more, she hated herself for contemplating such a stupid idea. Actually, the idea wasn't stupid, but the execution certainly was. She should have shot him at the first opportunity, cut his throat and been gone. But no, she had to have a conversation with the man. In disgust with herself, she closed her eyes, shook her head, and clenched her fists until her nails cut into her palms.

Edwards fondled her breast with one hand a few seconds before tossing Karen to the bunk. The stench flooded her nostrils as she scrambled to get back to her feet.

Just as she planted both feet on the floor, Edwards palmed her face with one hand and shoved her back down to the bunk. He shifted his hand to her chest to hold her down.

Karen was able to move her arms and feet, but it did little good against the strength in his one arm. She was pinned to the mattress with what felt like a ton of bricks.

That's when she remembered the knife strapped to her hip. With her hands free, she felt for the knife's hilt, found it, and whisked the blade from its sheath.

As she brought the blade around to go for his chest, his free hand suddenly shot out and wrapped around her wrist. She wriggled and struggled against his grip, but it was to no avail as his grip on her wrist tightened to the point of nearly breaking the bones. She finally relented, let loose her hold on the knife, and let it drop.

The knife bounced once on the edge of the bunk and then clanged to the floor.

"You're just full of surprises, aren't you?" he grunted. "Got any more hidden under those pants?"

While still holding her down with a stiff arm to the chest, he used the other hand to fiddle with her belt buckle. "Never seen a buckle like this one," he said, as he continued.

She used both hands to parry his efforts, but again, his strength was too much.

Edwards, still working with one hand, finally figured out the belt, undid the hasp, and immediately pulled at the pants flap until all the buttons tore loose, exposing Karen's bare skin. The sight of her milky white flesh invigorated him even more to pull at her pants until they were down to her knees.

Karen fought his every move with both hands, knees, and feet. She even tried to bite the stiff-arm still planted on her chest, but was not able to raise her head far enough. She screamed, wriggled, struggled, and pounded but it did no good. The very thing she'd intended to prevent was happening. The only difference, it was happening much sooner than expected. She thought of Mason and the others, all probably dead. She thought of Lisa and Michael, alone on the plantation—alone until some group of marauders or band of renegade Indians came along. In the end, she lasted only a few years longer than all the other survivors from the airline ditching. This time and place had proved too much to endure.

Karen snapped out of her reverie when she realized Edwards was pawing at her pubic mound. He ran his filthy fingers between her legs, despite her bucking hips. "You sorry son-of-a-bitch," she screamed, "you will die for this, maybe not by my hand, but you will die."

His only response was a glance at her face, reluctant to tear his focus away from his hand on and in her vagina. He paused a moment, glanced again at her upper torso, and then quickly released the pressure on her chest long enough to rip the shirt open straight down to the hem. Wearing nothing underneath, both breasts popped into view.

In the dimness of the room, there was just enough light to see the outline of his face. There was a glint on his chin, a wetness. She realized he was drooling as he worked both hands over her body.

He continually swept his tongue around his lips and grunted unintelligible moans. He worked one hand between her legs and at the same time fondled one breast with his fingers as he used the palm of his hand to keep her pinned.

She closed her eyes and tried to think. She swept her hands over the parts of the mattress she could reach, in search of anything that could be used as a weapon. There was nothing. She suddenly realized his hand was no longer between her legs. She blinked her eyes open and saw why. His lower body was only a silhouette, but she could tell that he was working the buttons of his own breeches. She saw them fall from his waist, exposing his own nakedness. As he turned at an angle, she could see the silhouette of his erection.

He paused, apparently realizing it would be impossible to enter her from on top with her pants still wrapped around her knees. The easier solution would have been to flip her over, but he didn't do that. Instead, he struggled with her pants, trying to pull them the rest of the way off. This proved difficult, given she continued to buck her hips and kick her feet in all directions, including at him.

He pulled, tugged, and tore with his one free hand, but the pants proved difficult to remove. "You're going to make this difficult, I see. That's fine, I like it that way. It prolongs the anticipation."

Her response was to kick harder, scratch at the arm and hand on her chest, and spew a long line of obscenities. She knew she would eventually lose, but she wasn't giving up until she exerted every ounce of energy she had left.

After a few moments of struggle, on both their parts, he finally was able to remove the pants from one leg. One leg was good enough. With her still bucking, he maneuvered himself around, held her now completely naked legs apart, and began to lower himself.

With much of his weight now on top of her, and using both hands to restrain her arms, she felt the tip of his penis probing for the right spot. His weight made it more and more impossible for her to move her torso and pelvis. His weight increased and the probing continued until he was there.

She closed her eyes and screamed, expecting his penis to plunge inside. Several moments passed and still he did not enter her, even though he had the right spot and angle. Then she felt his penis slide between her legs as his weight on top of her suddenly increased, making it difficult to take a breath. That's when she realized he was no longer moving and no longer grunting. In fact, he was no longer breathing. His head and body lay limp on top of her.

Just as she was about to panic at not being able to breathe, the weight suddenly lifted. She felt him roll to one side and heard a loud *thud* as his body hit the floor. With the weight gone, she was able to take a deep breath as she focused her eyes on the dark form standing over her.

"We must go," she heard Mato whisper.

Her first thought should have been to cover herself, but it wasn't. "Where the hell were you?" she screamed, as she raised up, still completely naked.

"Men on street," he said, "not able to come in until they leave."

She clenched her jaw tight, shook her head, and closed her eyes for several moments as she tried to get control of her anger. *It wasn't his fault; it was mine.* "You were there, outside? You saw him carry me inside?"

"I at end of street. I wait long time before I see you and Edwards in the street. He carry you inside. Men come near me. Night watch men. I not able to come out of hiding until now."

"You didn't hear me screaming?"

"I hear waves from river; not hear you scream until men go and I come inside."

Karen swung her legs over the edge of the bunk, intending to stand. But her feet landed on the bare skin of Edwards' thighs. She jerked her feet back to the bunk. "What did you do to him?"

"He dead," Mato said without emotion.

She exhaled and took her first calm breath. "Thank you. I'm glad you didn't wait where I said."

Mato grunted.

Karen stepped over the corpse at her feet, put her right foot back into the pants leg, and pulled the pants up to her waist. She fumbled with the flap until she realized all but two of the buttons were missing. She buttoned the two and then used the belt to cinch the pants tight around her waist, holding the flap in place. She pulled the shirt's torn edges together until they overlapped and tucked the shirt's hem into her pants. The shirt gaped open at the top, exposing plenty of skin and cleavage, but it wouldn't be that noticeable in the dark. She then thought of the walk she would have to make through town. "How long before sunup?"

"Soon, we go now."

She looked down at Edwards. "We can't leave him like this," she said, as she bent down. "Help me pull his pants up."

The two of them rolled him back and forth, working the pants up to his waist. She refastened his flap and the waist buttons of his breeches. She put her fingers on his neck to check for a pulse. She found none. She did find a massive amount of blood, but not from a cut throat. She felt around until her fingers came upon the knife, her knife, protruding from the base of his skull, with the blade angled up. He would have died instantly when the blade penetrated his brain.

She next patted down his body until she felt a pouch still attached to his waistband. The pouch jingled with coins. She withdrew the knife from his neck and used it to cut away the pouch. "We'll take this. Make it look like a robbery." She stood up with the knife in one hand and the pouch in the other. "Where's my satchel and pistol?"

"I leave on bar."

Karen scanned the room. Not seeing much in the dark, she took a moment to think, to ensure she wasn't forgetting anything that would tie her or Mato to the scene. Satisfied, she turned toward the doorway. "Let's go," she said, as she marched through the opening.

CHAPTER 20

Through most of the night, Mason watched Thomas go from one crew member to the next. In each case, they huddled, sometimes with three or four members together, and talked in whispers.

Mason had read somewhere that voting among all members of the crew was the predominate manner of major decision-making among pirates of this era. The crew could even outvote the captain in some cases. Mason had not seen that among this crew; all the decisions thus far had been made by Low. But since they outnumbered him nearly forty to one, it seemed reasonable to expect that, at some point, they might exercise some resistance.

It wasn't until Thomas came to Mason that Mason found out the reason for all the secrecy. Most members had had enough of Captain Low. His abandonment of Harris, his murder of Knob the quartermaster, and his general brutality, had become too much. Thomas explained there would be a vote come sunrise. He also explained that, as second in command, he was taking a big chance. While the vast majority had apparently sided with Thomas' view of things, only the actual vote, in the presence of Low, counted. And pirate crew members were known to change their mind with the cold stare of the captain, especially with a man like Low. If the members voted with Low, Thomas couldn't guarantee the outcome for those who voted against him.

"I've been with the crew a very short time," Mason said. "I get a vote?"

"Everyone on this crew gets a vote. It's part of the terms everyone agreed to when they joined the crew."

Mason didn't recall seeing any terms, or agreeing to anything, when he was brought on board. Apparently, Low and Thomas had forgotten.

"So, can I count on your vote?"

Mason had hoped to kill Low himself, but watching the crew do it would be almost as good. "Of course, you have my vote."

Thomas patted Mason on the shoulder and then moved off to the next man, leaving Mason standing in the middle of the cargo deck.

Low wasn't the only one responsible for the atrocities carried out against his fellow airline survivors that day on the original sloop. There were others among this crew that needed to die. But killing the entire crew was too much to hope for. He thought of McGregor and Thomas. He didn't recognize either one of them from that day. But even if they were members of the crew then, Low was the one primarily responsible. And he was the only one Mason was sure was on the schooner's deck that day.

It had been three years. But his final images of Manny, Dorothy, and all the others were burned into his consciousness like he had witnessed the events the day before. He missed them all. Even Nathan, in a way. Despite all his conniving, he had been whirled into the past through no fault of his own, just like all the others. And he did contribute on occasion. The only thing Mason could do for them at this point was kill the man responsible for destroying their lives. And finally, it looked as though Low might get the justice he deserved.

◆◆◆

Karen and Mato were back home as the eastern sky began to brighten.

Despite paddling against the current, Mato had made record time.

When the canoe was within reach, Karen grabbed hold of the dock and pulled the canoe the rest of the way. She stepped out and secured the bow line to one of the posts. She stood up straight, stretched her back, and rubbed at her weary eyes. She turned to Mato when he stepped onto the dock. "Thank you, Mato. I would be dead right now if it were not for you."

He tightened his lips and gave a simple nod. He then reached back into the canoe and retrieved his musket and Karen's satchel.

She took the satchel, gave a weak smile, and turned toward the house. "I'm dog tired, my friend. I'll see you later in the day."

Mato grunted an acknowledgement.

When she was halfway to the house, the back door opened and Lisa sprang through the opening. She raced toward Karen.

"I've been up all night, waiting for you. I thought you were dead or under arrest."

"It could have gone either of those directions; almost did," Karen said, as she let the satchel drop to the ground. She stepped forward and the two of them embraced.

In the dull light of early morning, Lisa stepped back while still holding Karen's shoulders with both hands. Her eyes grew wide when her gaze fell on Karen's shirt, which was gapped open, exposing the side of both breasts. "What happened to you?"

"A close call." She glanced at Mato, walking away from them, toward the work barn. "He saved my life."

Lisa covered her mouth with one hand as she took another step back, releasing Karen's shoulders. She scanned Karen's body from head to foot, paying particular attention to the torn pant's flap held in place with the belt. "Did he—"

"He got his hands on me."

"And that's all?"

Karen's eyes began to moisten. She closed them to stem the flow but it did no good. Tears ran down her cheeks.

Lisa wrapped her arms around her. "You need some rest. We can talk about this later." She picked up the satchel and guided Karen to the house.

Inside Karen's room, Lisa sat her on the edge of the bed. "Do you need help with anything?"

"I can manage," Karen said.

"Call out if you need anything."

"I'm good, I just need to come to terms with all that happened. I'll explain it all, later."

Lisa patted Karen on the shoulder and then exited the room, closing the door behind her.

Karen stood up, wiggled the shirt off her shoulders, and let it drop to the floor. She undid the belt and let it and the pants slide down her legs, and then stepped out of her shoes. She walked to the other side of the bed, picked up her shift from a straight-back chair, and slipped the long, linen shirt over her head. She then rolled into bed, slipped under the covers, and rolled to her side. It took some time, but she finally fell asleep.

◆◆◆

After getting a couple of hours' sleep, Mason stepped up on the main deck to find most of the crew already there. The sails were furled, leaving the ship to undulate with the moderate waves and light breeze. The crew members stood around, talking among themselves in small groups. Mason ambled over to McGregor and Thomas, standing together amidships. "Time to vote?"

"It is," McGregor said. "Just waiting on the captain."

Mason glanced at the still-closed hatch to the captain's cabin, in the stern. "You going to wake him?"

"Nah, we can wait," Thomas said, as he scanned the others on deck.

"So, what happens if he's voted out as captain?" Mason asked.

McGregor shuffled his feet. "The better question is what happens if he's not."

Thomas raised an eyebrow.

"What will happen?"

"He can't kill all of us," McGregor said with a smirk.

"There won't be any killing," Thomas said.

At that moment, the hatch swung open and Low climbed out. "Why are we stopped?" he yelled. "Who gave the order to furl those sails?" He did a three-sixty survey of the ocean. Seeing nothing but water to the horizon in every direction, he focused on Thomas.

"Why are we stopped?" he asked, as he marched up and stood toe-to-toe.

Thomas' jaw muscles flexed as he glanced back at the other crew members, now on their feet, and focused on Thomas. "I called for a vote."

Low stepped back and surveyed the crew. His eyes paused on several he could usually count on.

The crew member's expressions remained neutral, except for a couple who turned their gaze to the deck.

Low turned back to Thomas. "A vote about me? About my ability to captain this ship?"

Thomas nodded.

"Harris and Knob brought this on?" Low asked, as he peered into Thomas' eyes for several moments. He finally broke the gaze and shuffled to the center of the deck, to address all the men. "Harris would have done the same thing. We had no chance against that frigate. As captain, it was my decision. I made it. As for Knob, the thieving bastard took from all of us."

"That was never proven," Thomas said. "We searched his belongings and found nothing."

"That proves nothing," Low shouted. "He hid it somewhere on this vessel." He turned back to Thomas. "Did you search every inch of this ship?"

Thomas took a deep breath and exhaled without responding.

"I thought not," Low said. "You would have found the silver if you had."

"How can you be so sure?" Thomas asked.

"I know men, and I knew Knob very well." Low moved his chin up and down. "He took the silver, and it's still hidden on this ship."

"Maybe you hid the silver after you killed him," McGregor said.

Low focused on McGregor's eyes. "I never would have thought you'd turn agin' me."

"You shouldn't have killed Knob," McGregor said. "He was a member of the crew. The articles we all signed says a member won't kill another member."

"Without good reason," Low said. "I had good reason."

"We're here to vote," Thomas said. "That will decide if you had good reason. What about Harris? We had sail, and we had working guns."

"Like I said, my decision. If we had fired, we just as likely would have hit Ranger. I made the only reasonable decision." He turned in an arc to address the entire crew. "I've captained you men for months, some for years. Have I ever let you down? Have we ever lost a fight?"

Several adjusted their stances. Some looked at each other.

"The answer is no," Low spat. "Not once. You men are alive today because of me."

"A lot of us are dead because of you," Thomas said. "Including Knob and likely Harris, soon, if he ain't already." Thomas turned to address the crew. "He takes too many chances with our lives. We lose too many because of his tactics." He turned back to Low. "You butcher people when it ain't necessary."

"Who are you to decide what's necessary? I'm the captain, I decide."

"That's what we're here to vote on," McGregor said. "Each man will vote. The majority rules. It's the law."

The ship suddenly went quiet as everyone stared at Thomas and Low, standing in the middle of the deck.

"Do I need to remind you, this is my ship?" Low said. "In fact, Fortune, Ranger, and Fancy are all my ships. I'm the captain of all of them, and what I say goes."

"Ranger was either sunk or taken into port," Thomas said. "Fancy is likely in the tropics under Spriggs' command." Thomas looked around at the deck. His voice took on a newfound confidence. "This seems to be the only ship in question at the moment, and the way I see it, it belongs to the members currently occupying its decks."

"Fine," Low said calmly. "You want a vote, let's have a vote. I have all day," he said, as he took a seat on the captain's cabin hatch opening.

The watchman above in the crow's nest sang out. "Sails ho," he yelled.

Low got to his feet. "What is she?" he yelled up to the watchman.

"Single mast. A sloop."

Low looked at Thomas and then back up at the watchman. "The same one from before?"

"Barely visible on the horizon. Can't tell, but maybe."

"Speed and direction?" Thomas yelled.

"Sails are flapping. No speed; no direction. Directly on the beam."

"Guns?" Low yelled.

"Can't tell. Too far."

"I think we should explore that ghost ship, Mister Thomas," Low said.

Thomas stared off to beam and then back up at the watchman. "You say she's not moving?"

"Dead in the water. Sails are slack. She's just waiting there, Mister Thomas."

"Seems we have time for a vote," Mason said.

Everyone, but especially Low, Thomas, and McGregor, jerked their heads to Mason, apparently surprised he had said anything.

"I'm just saying," Mason said, "we're here for a vote, we have time, let's vote."

Thomas pursed his lips as he nodded. He turned to McGregor. "Prepare the ballots, McGregor. And something to write with. I want a record of this vote, either way."

McGregor ambled off and disappeared through the cargo hatch.

"With a ship on our beam," Low said, "really think we should take the time for a vote?"

"I do," Thomas said, "and so do they." He motioned to the crew members, none of whom had moved from their positions.

"Keep an eye on that ship," Low yelled to the watchman. "Sing out if she moves."

◆◆◆

"What in the hell are they doing?" Jeremy asked, as he squinted at the sloop in the far distance.

"Just sitting there," Forrest said. "We were in view of her watchman before I realized they were heaving to."

"They can see us?"

"Without a doubt," Forrest said.

Charlie crawled out of the small cabin below deck and joined Jeremy and Forrest. "What is it?" he asked, as he looked where they were looking. "Is that Low's ship?"

"One of the two," Forrest said. "I've had their lantern in sight for hours. They suddenly heaved to about an hour ago. Sails are furled. They're just sitting there."

Jeremy turned to Charlie. "Any idea why they would do that? Just sit there?"

Charlie shook his head. "Don't know. They certainly wouldn't do that if there was a ship in sight, a potential target."

"We're in sight, and they're still not moving."

"That is a curious one," Charlie said. "They know we're small and of little threat. Whatever they're doing must be more important."

Jeremy dropped his chin toward the deck and pinched the bridge of his nose. "How are we doing on water?"

"Drank the last of it yesterday. We have a bit of rum left. No food."

"This might be a good time to head for the coast," Forrest said.

Charlie looked at Jeremy for a response.

"Us dying of thirst won't help Mason," Forrest said.

Jeremy stared at Forrest for several moments before finally tightening his lips with a slight nod.

CHAPTER 21

McGregor returned with scraps of paper and a few lumps of charcoal. He placed the items on the hatch cover.

"Mark an 'X' if he goes, a single line if he stays," Thomas said. He picked up a piece of paper, a charcoal, and marked an 'X' in full view of Low and the crew. He removed the hat from a nearby crew member and dropped the paper inside. "Completed ballots go here."

Each man in turn stepped up. Most took the paper and charcoal away, to be marked in private. But a few marked the paper in view of Low.

When it was Mason's turn, he took his paper and charcoal to the base of the main mast, away from other crew members. He marked an 'X', folded the paper, and ambled back up to Thomas. He dropped the paper inside the hat without comment, turned away, and found a spot at the port gunwale to observe. He watched the voting process for a few moments but then turned his attention to the horizon, to the spot where the watchman saw the single-masted ship. There was nothing in sight, given his angle of view. He glanced to the watchman and saw him take a final look at the horizon and then begin to climb down.

The watchman voted and then scampered back up the rat line to his perch. "No change in the ship's position," he yelled down.

When the last few men had dropped their ballots into the hat, Thomas took a seat on the hatch cover. He pointed to a nearby crew member and handed him a blank piece of paper and a bit of charcoal. "Keep track as I call them out." He turned to McGregor. "We need a witness as I check the ballots."

McGregor stepped up and stood next to Thomas.

Low took a seat at the base of the mast and faced Thomas. His expression remained neutral. He knew there was little he could do at this point. His fate was in the hands of the crew.

Thomas pulled the first piece of paper from the hat and unfolded it. "For," he announced. "Meaning he stays." He handed the paper to McGregor.

McGregor glanced at the paper and nodded.

Thomas pulled the next paper and read the vote. "Agin'." He handed the paper McGregor.

McGregor nodded.

Halfway through the tally the vote was even. Given the allegations against Low, Mason was surprised that so many would side with him. But then, as Low pointed out, some of these men had been with him for years.

Three-quarters of the way through, the tally was eleven against and thirteen for, meaning Low had the majority in his favor, with only eight votes to go.

Mason leaned closer to the nearest crew member. "What happens with a tie?" he whispered.

"Tie goes to the accused," the man mumbled.

Mason suddenly realized that he had not seen Low cast a vote. That meant he would have to lose by two votes to be removed as captain.

"For," Thomas announced. He handed the paper to McGregor.

McGregor nodded.

Low was two votes ahead and he still had his own vote to cast.

Thomas pulled the next piece of paper. His eyes widened just before he read the vote, "For."

That left six votes to go and Low was four votes ahead.

Thomas unfolded the next paper. "The vote is—" he paused for affect, "—against." He handed the paper to McGregor.

He unfolded the next five pieces of paper in succession and read the vote before handing each to McGregor.

"Does any member wish for the votes to be tallied again?" Thomas asked, as he got to his feet.

When no one commented, Low got to his feet. He scanned the crew members and spent several moments peering into each man's eyes. He finally looked at Thomas and McGregor, standing together at the hatch. "It seems the crew has decided. I must say, I am surprised at you gentlemen."

Thomas stepped forward. "The crew has voted and a clear decision has been rendered," he announced loud enough for everyone to hear, even the watchman above. He turned to Low. "Edward Low, you are hereby removed as captain and you must disembark this vessel immediately."

Low motioned with his hand. "In the middle of the ocean?"

"You'll be given the jolly boat, food, and water. Nothing else." He turned to the crew. "Does any man object?"

No one made a sound.

"Everything I've done, I've done for this crew," Low said with a steady voice.

"Everything you've done, you did for you," Thomas said. "The murder of Knob and the abandonment of Harris—"

"Yes, yes, so you've said," Low said. "My sword and pistol?"

Thomas shook his head as he stared at Low. He turned to the crew. "One more thing. Anyone who wishes, is free to go with Ned. You'll be given plenty of food and water. You should reach land in a few days." He turned in a slow arc, looking for a sign from any who might want to go. His eyes reached the last of the men, Mason. He was about to turn away, obviously expecting him to decline, when Mason took a step forward. Thomas refocused on Mason's face and cocked his head.

McGregor came to attention, with his eyes locked on Mason as well.

Every member of the crew turned to Mason.

"I'll be going with Ned," Mason announced.

◆◆◆

"Is there any more coffee?" Karen asked as she entered the common dining area and saw Lisa sitting with Mato. The area was otherwise empty in the mid-morning, except for Marie attending to something at the hearth. Probably working on dinner.

Lisa patted the bench next to her. "Have a seat," she said, as she got to her feet. "I'll get you some coffee."

Karen sat as Lisa walked off toward Marie and the cooking area. "Did you get any sleep?" Karen asked Mato.

"Sleep at night," Mato said.

"Thank you again for last night. I was an idiot to think I could handle him on my own."

"What idiot mean?"

"It means I wasn't thinking very well."

"Thinking very well about what?" Lisa asked, as she took her seat next to Karen. She slid a mug of steaming coffee in front of Karen.

"Last night. You were right."

Lisa glanced at Mato. "How far did Edwards get? You never said. Are you really alright?"

"He came within a millimeter of me feeling dirty the rest of my life," Karen said. She looked at Mato and smiled.

"Thanks to him, I only have to feel a little bit dirty."

"I take it Mato intervened just in time."

"Another second and things would have been much different for me."

"Will there be questions by the authorities?" Lisa asked.

"I'm sure, but there's nothing to tie us to Edwards."

Sylvester poked his head in the doorway. "Excuse me, Miss Karen, there's men at the dock. Three of them."

Karen stared at Mato.

"You two wait here, I'll take care of this," Lisa said as she got to her feet. She joined Sylvester at the door and the two of them started off across the yard.

"Men come for Mato?" he asked, looking at Karen.

"It's probably not related, but you may want to stay in here, just in case." She turned her gaze to the open doorway and watched as three men approached

Lisa and Sylvester. The five of them came to a stop about halfway to the dock. Karen recognized the provost marshal, Mister Loughton. He was doing most of the talking. The butterflies in her stomach started to rumble.

Karen got to her feet. "You wait here, Mato. I'll go see what's going on."

Mato grunted.

Loughton stopped talking when Karen stepped from the doorway and began walking in their direction.

"What is this about?" Karen asked as she came to a stop next to Lisa.

"I was just explaining," Loughton said, "we had a killing last night in town. Mister Edwards from the tavern."

Shivers reverberated through Karen's body, but she did a good job of maintaining a calm outward appearance. "And what does that have to do with us?"

"Your friend, Mato, was seen in town last night. With another man. Unknown at the moment. Is this Mato staying here with you?"

"He is," Karen said. "But to my knowledge, he hasn't been in town lately. Is your witness sure it was Mato?"

"Who can be a hundred percent sure at night, in the dim light," Loughton said, "but Mato was named."

"Other than possibly seeing him in town, which is not likely, what makes you think Mato was involved with Edwards being dead? How did he die?"

"Appears to be a knife to the brain."

"And why is Mato a suspect?"

"They had a falling out recently. But you know that, you were the one who intervened on Mato's behalf."

"Killing someone over some pelts, a situation that was resolved, seems rather farfetched," Karen said.

"Maybe, but he's a suspect nonetheless. Is he around?"

Karen turned to Lisa. "Could you see if he's about and ask him to join us?"

Lisa stared at Karen until she received a subtle nod and then pivoted and walked off.

Karen turned back to Loughton. "Last night, you say, in the dark." Karen twisted her lips. "That seems odd. I have no reason, as I said, to think he was in town last night. That's all you have; someone saw an Indian? There are many of them about. Quite friendly, at least presently. That could probably change. Wouldn't take much, especially with a man like Mato. He's held in very high regard among the Catawba, as you probably know."

Loughton's expression remained neutral and he didn't comment. After a few moments, his eyes focused on something behind Karen.

She glanced back at Lisa and Mato approaching. Karen was thankful Lisa had apparently convinced Mato to remove his feather headdress, something a witness might remember.

"You want to talk to Mato?" he asked, as he and Lisa came to a stop next to Karen. He kept his gaze steady on Loughton's eyes.

Loughton studied Mato from head to toe. His expression suddenly softened, apparently concluding Mato could in fact be confused with any other brave of his approximate size and shape. "Have you been in town lately?" he finally asked.

"Go town many times."

"What about last night?"

"I here last night," Mato said with confidence.

That technically wasn't a lie. He was at the plantation the previous evening, at least part of the evening.

"Really, Mister Loughton," Karen said, "Mato is a close friend of this family. He's traded in town for years and, from what I understand, there was a disagreement with Edwards every time he went into the tavern. That was Edwards' nature, from what I gather, at least, that's the impression I got when I dealt with him. It's part of doing business with the Edwards tavern. It was, anyway. There must be a great many people who were unhappy with the way Edwards treated them."

Loughton listened intently. When Karen finished talking, he simply pursed his lips as he continued to stare at her. He glanced at Mato, back to Karen, and then he scanned the plantation.

"Have you determined a motive?"

Loughton turned back to Karen. "Motive?"

"Why was he killed?"

Loughton took in a deep breath, exhaled, and cocked his head. "Appears to have been a robbery. Woody says his money pouch was missing. He always wore it on his waist."

"Well, just because someone saw an Indian in town, you suspect he was robbed for his money by an Indian?"

Loughton glanced at Mato. "Like I said, the two of them had a disagreement that landed Mato in the holding cell. That's a little more serious than their typical disagreement."

"As I said, that was resolved," Karen said. "I was there. Edwards seemed perfectly happy with our arrangement when Mato and I left him. And that was days ago."

Loughton's chin began to subtly move up and down.

"Is there anything else we can help you with, Mister Loughton?" Karen asked.

Loughton scanned the plantation again. "No word from Mason, I take it?"

"None at all," Lisa said. "And Jeremy, Forrest, and Charlie haven't returned either."

"Frankly, I'm more than a little worried," Karen said. "Our men are out there, risking their lives, for you."

"Well, for the governor," Loughton said. He took a final look around and glanced at Mato again. "I guess I've taken up enough of your time." He raised two fingers to the brim of his hat, pivoted, motioned for his two men to follow, and walked off toward the dock.

CHAPTER 22

"Are you sure you want to do that?" Thomas asked, as he stared at Mason.

"It's a chance to return home," Mason said. "You'll recall, I wasn't really expecting to become a member of this crew when I escaped with Libby from Charlestown."

"Every member of this crew is free to come and go as they want," Thomas said. He glanced at Low. "At least, they are now. You can depart our company at our next port."

"That might be a good ways from my home," Mason said. "I'd prefer to depart now."

"The man made his decision," Low said. "And he's welcome to join me."

"Suit yourself," Thomas said to Mason. He faced McGregor. "We'll need the jolly boat readied and provisions placed on board."

Low cleared his voice. "Just curious, did I miss the vote making you captain?"

"There will be another vote as soon as you and Mason have disembarked."

Low surveyed the crew. Finding no objections, he nodded at Thomas. "Hope you know what you're doing," he said, as he swept his arm in an arc. "For their sake."

Outfitted with four oars, they lowered the jolly boat into the water using a block and tackle. They provisioned it with two small kegs of water, a keg of rum, biscuits, and boiled salt pork.

Low and Mason climbed down, pushed away from the sloop, and began pulling at the oars.

Nearly every crew member stood at the port gunwale, bow to stern, to watch the notorious Edward Low assume his latest command.

Some members of the crew smirked, but most simply stared as Low and Mason worked the oars.

It was nearing noon, with the sun high in the sky, but the air was cool with a light breeze. Mason was thankful for his coat and hat. They would keep most of the sun from his skin.

From about three hundred yards out, Mason watched the sails being hoisted on Fortune. Within minutes, the sloop was on a southerly heading, probably making for the Bahama Islands.

Mason looked up at the sun and then glanced back at Low, seated behind him. "Which direction are we headed?"

"North. The east coast is still the nearest land mass."

"Sounds fine by me," Mason said.

"We need to get something straight," Low said. "I'm in charge of this little excursion. And my top priority is to acquire another ship and head south. If you're on board with that plan, you're welcome to join in. If not, you can depart my company any time you want."

"Understood," Mason said. Mason had a plan of his own but, for now, two people rowing was better than one. He doubted Jeremy, if that was Jeremy on the horizon, would have seen the jolly boat being offloaded, much less two men boarding the tiny craft. Even if they had, they would have been faced with a dilemma. Follow the sloop, or go after the jolly boat. Doing the latter would have meant losing sight of the sloop. Mason wasn't sure what he would have done in that situation. Frankly, he would be surprised if that was Jeremy in the sloop on the horizon. If it was, they had been at sea for nearly two weeks, and had to have been running out of food and water. Chances were, Jeremy headed back to shore days earlier, and that assumed he had been able to acquire Low's sloop to begin with. For now, Mason's best option was to row north and let Low be in charge.

"How long do you expect this will take?" Mason asked.

"At least three days. And while we're rowing north, the currents will be sweeping us east. Not sure where we'll end up. Perhaps we'll be picked up."

Mason hoped not. The last thing Mason wanted was for Low to get a chance at another ship. He was just one man, but based on what Mason had researched about Low, that one man had accomplished a lot in a short period of time, and had survived numerous close calls.

"Will you chase down Thomas?" Mason asked.

"If the opportunity were to arise, Thomas might would meet the end of my sword, but I won't chase him. The crew voted. That's that."

"Someone told me you were married once."

"None of anybody's business," Low said, "and certainly none of yours."

They rowed in relative silence for the next hour. Low took frequent breaks, each an opportunity to sip some of the rum, which was fine by Mason. He could drink all the rum he wanted, as long as he didn't waste the water.

Mason wasn't lost on the fact that he currently had Low right where he had always hoped. Alone. He often thought about what he would do to the man, should the opportunity present itself. Images of Dorothy and Manny flashed through his mind, along with Karen and Michael, hopefully safe at the plantation. He scanned the ocean in all directions and saw nothing but water. Sitting this low to the surface, he estimated his range of view was only about five or six miles. He began to wonder about Low, and whether he could trust the man, especially when Mason slept. Mason gave the situation a lot of thought and finally came to a decision.

Mason secured his oars and picked up one of the kegs of water. He removed the plug and took a swig. He replaced the cork, returned the keg to its place with the rest of the stores, and spun around on his bench to face Low. "We met once," he said, wiping his mouth with the back of his hand.

Low stopped rowing, secured his oars, and picked up the keg of rum. "Really, when?" He took a swig of the rum.

"About three years ago, off the Carolina coast. I was on a sloop with a group of people. Friends of mine. We were headed for a new life."

Low took another swig, replaced the plug, and set the keg at his feet. "A sloop, you say? Carolina coast?"

"That's right."

"I don't recall, but I've come in contact with a great many ships on the seas." He stared at Mason and ran his eyes head to foot. "You seem to have survived our encounter."

"There were only two of us survived that day," Mason said, as he let his eyes penetrate Low's soul.

Low's eyes suddenly flashed with recollection. He stared at Mason for several long moments.

Mason could see the wheels turning.

"My silver," Low finally said. "You had my silver."

Mason nodded.

"You should have heaved to. I would have taken my property and left you in peace."

"I doubt that."

"As I recall, there was no one left alive on that sloop when we departed."

"That's true. I wasn't on the sloop. I was blasted into the water with one of your first cannon blasts."

"I remember you," Low said. "You fired at me from behind the mast."

Mason tightened his lips and nodded.

"You were one man, but you fired many times. I always wondered about that."

"Let me set your mind at ease. You see, my friends and I were not from here. We weren't even from this time."

Low's eyes squinted. "Not from this time." A broad smile spread across his face.

Mason continued. "That's right, my friends and I were hurled back through time from a distant future, a future when firearms are much more powerful than what you have now."

Low broke out laughing, a long belly laugh.

Mason maintained a dead serious stare.

Tears of laughter ran down Low's cheeks as he got control of himself. "I must say, Mister Mason, you can spin an interesting yarn. I appreciate that. Helps pass the time."

"How do you explain fifteen or so shots in that many seconds?"

Low's expression turned more serious. "You actually expect me to believe you came from the future?"

"I downed several of your men, including the one standing next to you."

Low stared at Mason for a full twenty seconds. Finally, he spoke, "This is hogwash." He stared at Mason a few seconds more. "I, of course, don't believe you came from the future, but I'd like to see this firearm you speak of."

"That's never going to happen. That's the reason I'm here."

More recollection spread over Low's face. "You were put in that cell with Libby."

"I volunteered. In fact, it was my idea."

"I wasn't alone that day on the ocean," Low said.

"You were the one in command. It was your ruthlessness, and yours alone, that resulted in the massacre of my friends."

"So, you planned this whole thing, just to get this opportunity, with me, here, alone?"

"That's right."

Low scanned the water in all directions.

"That sloop on our stern the last few days."

"More of my friends," Mason said.

"And Thomas? The vote?"

"Pure happenstance. Wasn't part of my plan but it fit in nicely, wouldn't you say?"

"There's one flaw in this plan of yours." He stared at Mason for a reaction. He didn't get one. "What makes you think you can take me? Neither of us have weapons. At the moment, it's just the two of us."

Mason stared into Low's eyes without responding.

Low clenched his teeth. His jaw flexed. He suddenly lunged at Mason with balled fists.

He was quicker than Mason expected, but not quick enough. He ducked, letting the first blow pass harmlessly above his head.

Low's momentum propelled his body forward, crashing into Mason, sending them both to the bottom of the boat and into the few inches of water it held. With moans, groans, and a tangle of arms and legs, the two of them wrestled. With Low on top, he managed to throw a few punches to Mason's rib cage, but much of their power was lost to the lack of leverage. In the tight space between the bench and the transom, neither man could gain the advantage as they sloshed around in the water.

Mason had, in fact, underestimated Low's strength. There was some muscle hiding behind that extra layer of fat around his midsection. Plus, despite being shorter, he outweighed Mason by at least ten pounds. Given the lack of space to maneuver, Mason was finding it nearly impossible to get the man off of him. The best he could do at the moment was to wrap both arms around Low's neck, tuck his head in, and keep his elbows folded to block the blows.

From his position on top, Low flailed his fists. Most landed with a glancing blow, having first lost much of their power on Mason's upper arms. With Low unable to raise his own head, he couldn't get an angle on Mason's face. With his legs, Low tried to raise his torso, but each time he did, Mason simply increased the pressure on the back of his neck. Low had to let his body flop back on top of Mason, rather than risk a broken neck.

After several minutes of this, Low began losing steam. His punches lacked the power they'd had initially and he was breathing hard. He finally stopped punching and began trying to wrest Mason's arms from around his neck.

Mason thought of letting go but decided against it. His arms around the neck was working to subdue Low. Low was fatiguing much faster than Mason. It was true what they said. With most fights, the combatants end up on the ground within about ten seconds. For that reason, Mason had studied Jujutsu while in the army, and continued lessons while working as an air marshal. He knew a great many grappling techniques. But he saw no reason to change his current tactic. The more exasperated Low became, the more quickly he would expend his energy.

Low began slamming his knees into Mason's thighs, but they did little damage. With his palms against the bottom of the boat on either side of Mason, he tried lifting Mason in the air. That succeeded, but only by a few inches. When Low tried pounding Mason's back to the bottom of the boat, it, too, did little damage. The few inches of water that had accumulated helped soften the blow. Then Low tried rolling to one side and then the other. That, too, failed. With each attempt, Mason simply placed a foot against the side of the boat to counter Low's leverage and weight.

Mason held on, increasing the pressure each time Low tried a different maneuver.

Low finally stopped flailing around with his fists and legs. He had lost much of his energy and went mostly limp as he gasped for air.

Mason suddenly released his arms from around Low's neck and pushed him up with his hands while he brought his knees to his chest. He got his feet on Low's chest and then pushed with all his might.

Low catapulted up and back. His calves caught the edge of the bench, which caused him to pivot in midair and crash down to the bottom of the boat. His back slammed into the hull with a loud *thump* and a splash of water.

Mason was immediately up. He scrambled over the bench, lifted Low's head, and placed him in a neck crank from behind as he wrapped both legs around Low's waist. He squeezed tightly.

Low grunted, flailed his arms, trying to grasp Mason's head, but was otherwise unable to do much of anything.

"The people on that sloop, my friends, didn't deserve to die that day. The last thing you will hear before you leave this earth is their names. The people you killed."

Low moaned and groaned while Mason spoke.

"They were Angie Knowles, Dorothy Weiss, Travis Turner, Manny Hernandez, Mildred Spears and her dog, Tito, Tom Green, Gail Thomas, Sandy Craven, Toby Wellen, Hana and Asumi, Koji, Lana Broadhurst, and John Tifton. And there was Nathan Sims. You took him aboard your ship to serve as a member of your crew, which he did. He was killed three years ago for his treachery."

"What do you expect me to say?" Low grunted.

"I don't expect anything from you," Mason said as he slowly increased the pressure on Low's neck, while using his upper body to twist.

Low's neck bent at an exaggerated angle until there was a loud *snap*. His body went instantly limp as a final breath flowed from his lungs.

Mason released his hold on the man's neck and let his upper body fall prostrate to the bottom of the boat. He leaned back against the gunwale as he stared at the now dead Edward Low. He contemplated taking his body to shore for the authorities to celebrate over, but decided against it. As he started to his feet, he heard a voice behind him. Jeremy's voice.

"You need a ride?"

Mason jerked his head around and saw the sloop with Jeremy, Charlie, and Forrest all at the bow staring down at him, not fifty feet away.

"Who's your friend?" Charlie asked.

Mason glanced at Low. "That is the former Edward Low, pirate extraordinaire."

"You did it," Jeremy exclaimed. "You killed Edward Low."

"It would seem," Mason said.

"You taking his body to the authorities?" Forrest asked.

Mason stared at the corpse for a few moments. He shook his head. "No. I don't need to prove anything to anyone." Mason got to his feet, grabbed Low under both armpits, and wrestled him to the gunwale. He lifted and pushed until Low's dead weight finally slid over the side and slipped into the waiting ocean. The body bobbed a couple of times and then slowly sank until he was out of sight.

"What about the jolly boat?" Charlie asked. "Looks to be in good shape."

"You're right," Mason said. "We can use it at the farm."

"Any chance you have some water?" Jeremy asked. "We've been out for over a day."

"Two kegs, some rum, biscuits, and boiled salt pork. Enough to get us home."

Charlie and Forrest helped Mason aboard while Jeremy held the jolly boat's bow line.

When Mason planted both feet on the deck, he paused and closed his eyes for several moments. He opened them to see his three friends staring at him. "I'm glad to be back on this boat and headed home."

"As are we all," Jeremy said.

CHAPTER 23

Mason was at the bow, with his eyes toward the setting sun, when Forrest sauntered up next to him.

"How bad was it?"

Mason glanced at him. "I wasn't treated badly, but having to witness Low's attacks on merchant ships was painful."

"What kind of people are they?"

"Some are downright demonic, but most are just lost souls." He turned and stared at Forrest. "I'm glad you hung around. Will you be heading back to New York?"

"If it's alright with you and the others, I was hoping to remain at the plantation."

"Of course you're welcome. You're a kindred soul. Someone who understands our situation. But what about your tavern? Your relationships?"

"I brought everything of value with me, so I have no need to return. I'll write and let Tom know."

"Tom?"

"The man I gave the key to."

"No budding relationships I take it?"

"None. There was someone a few years ago, but she enjoyed the whiskey more than my company."

Mason put a hand on Forrest's shoulder. "Like I said, you're welcome to stay as long as you want. I, for one, would very much enjoy your company. And we'll be making yearly trips to New York. You can stop in and say hello to Tom."

Forrest turned to face the sun, just passing below the horizon. "So, tell me, what are the women like in Charlestown?"

Mason smiled.

Late afternoon of the third day since picking up Mason, Charlestown harbor came into view.

"Are we stopping?" Jeremy asked.

"I think we need to fill Loughton in on what happened," Mason said. "Since we're here."

They maneuvered the sloop through the harbor and approached the wharves. By this time, Jeremy had become pretty much an expert at docking and was able to bring the sloop right up to the first available dock.

"That was amazing," Mason said. "Never seen a better job of docking a boat."

"Everyone going ashore?" Charlie asked.

"Absolutely," Mason replied. "We all need a good dinner. The muskets are the only thing of value. Bring 'em."

The four men marched down the wharves, into town, and straight to Loughton's home.

Mason knocked on the door.

The door swung open, revealing the provost marshal. He stood with his mouth open for several moments before finally speaking. "I thought for sure I'd never see you again."

"It was touch and go there for a while," Mason said with a smile.

"Touch and go," Loughton repeated. "Never heard that expression before."

"I can fill you in on everything if you have the time," Mason said.

Loughton opened the door wider and stepped to the side. "You'll all be staying for dinner, of course. About an hour or so." He pointed to a room immediately off the foyer. "Have a seat in my study. I'll let the misses know and join you shortly."

Mason led the others into the room, where they each found a seat.

Mason left a well-worn stuffed chair near the window empty. It was probably where Loughton sat and read.

Loughton returned and walked straight to an ornately designed bureau with a fold-down front displaying several bottles of spirits and various glasses. He selected five small port glasses, pulled a cork from one of the bottles, and filled the glasses. He handed out the port and then took a seat in the chair Mason had left empty. "Start from the very beginning. I want to hear every detail."

Mason began by introducing Forrest and then started his story with the time in the night watch holding cell with Libby. He detailed Low's arrival, the murder of the two night watchmen, the deliberation on whether Mason should be taken or killed, and boarding Low's ship, which Mason later learned was named the Fortune. He talked about his initial duties, the feeling that he could be killed at Low's least little whim, and finally being able to assimilate and becoming a member of a gun crew. He described the attacks on the several merchant ships they'd encountered, Low's brutality, and his own efforts to avoid doing anything that would have aided in the death of innocent civilians. He went into great detail about Low, described his appearance, his mannerisms, and his interaction with the crew. He described the rendezvous with Charles Harris aboard Ranger. He went into great detail about the battle with the royal frigate, Harris' defeat, Low's abandonment, and the impact of that decision on the rest of the crew. He talked about the murder of Knob, the quartermaster, and how that was apparently the last straw. He explained how he volunteered to go with Low when he was removed as captain, their fight aboard the jolly boat, and Low's death. After talking for nearly two hours, Mason finally stopped and looked at the faces looking back at him. All stared with amazed expressions.

"And you say Low's death was witnessed by the three of you?" Loughton asked, as his gaze traveled from Jeremy, Charlie, and Forrest.

"That's right," Jeremy said. "We were approaching when Mason broke his neck. We all watched him dump Low into the sea."

"Any idea where Thomas was headed after you and Low left the ship?" Loughton asked.

"They talked about the tropics, Nassau," Mason said. "Francis Spriggs, aboard the schooner Fancy, was supposed to have been in that area. As you know, Low, Harris, and Spriggs were closely aligned."

"Which is what surprises me about Low abandoning his friend Harris."

Mason nodded. "That apparently surprised a lot of people."

Misses Loughton came into the room for the fourth time to announce dinner would soon be stone cold.

Loughton got to his feet. "Gentlemen, please join us for dinner."

Mason and the others followed Loughton and his wife into the dining room and were met with a long table laid out with a large pot of a venison soup, fresh-made bread, cheese, and dried fruits.

Everyone took a seat while Misses Loughton ladled out the soup. Despite her claim, the soup was piping hot, having been kept that way on a hook in the hearth.

Over dinner, Jeremy, Charlie, and Forrest had a chance to describe their efforts to stay within sight of Low's ship without being detected.

"You were seen," Mason said. "The watchman spotted you. But the sloop was deemed too small to bother with."

"Good thing for you all, Low decided against investigating," Misses Loughton said.

Conversation continued back in the study over another glass or two of port for another two hours.

"It's getting late, gentlemen. You will, of course, be staying here tonight."

"Reminds me of the last time Jeremy and I spent the night in this house," Mason said.

"Much different circumstances," Loughton said. "By the way, I should mention that I suspected your friend Mato of killing Mister Edwards."

"Edwards?" Jeremy asked. "From the tavern?"

"One and the same," Loughton said.

"Suspected." Mason said. "So, you don't know for sure?"

"Your wife vouched for Mato. Without additional evidence, I'm inclined to let the matter rest. Edwards was a scoundrel. It was only a matter of time until he crossed the wrong man."

"And Mato?" Charlie asked. "He's no longer a suspect?"

Loughton rubbed the palms of his hands together as he peered at Charlie. "I have no quarrel with Mister Mato. For now. I do find it interesting that he was named as having been seen in town that night, only a few days after having had a falling out with Edwards." He flicked his hands in the air. "But as I said, I'm inclined to let it rest. Unless more evidence comes to light. Which I don't expect."

"Thank you," Mason said. "Mato is a very good friend. I find it hard to believe he would murder a man over a trade disagreement."

Loughton simply nodded as he got to his feet. "Gentlemen, let me show you to your rooms. In the morning, I think you should inform the governor personally."

◆◆◆

Early the next morning, the five men stood before Sir Francis Nicholson, the governor of the South Carolina Colony, in the study of his home at 65 Broad Street.

The house was larger than most, but did not rise to the level of a typical governor's mansion. Still, it was large enough to entertain up to fifty people comfortably, which the governor often did.

The governor himself was a large man and was seldom seen out of one of his dazzling, ornately adorned, long coats. Most were a shade of blue. His hair was dark, wavy, and long, to the middle of his back. He was known for his ill temper, which could be provoked in the blink of an eye.

Mason had made it a point to steer clear of the man, given that he and William Rhett were often at odds. It was well known that each had accused the other of smuggling, something never proven in either case. It was common to be accused of smuggling, something to which Mason could well attest.

Nicholson got to his feet and walked around to the front of his desk. "Mister Mason, I'm happy to see you in one piece."

"Thank you, sir. You'll be happy to know that Edward Low is no longer among the living. I killed him myself." He motioned to Charlie, Jeremy, and Forrest. "These men witnessed me dump the man's body into the sea."

"Marvelous," Nicholson said, as he clapped his hands together, "simply marvelous. You must tell me all about it." He motioned to a circle of chairs and settees in one corner of the large room. "Please, have a seat."

Mason went through the entire story again, abbreviating parts he thought wouldn't be of much interest to the governor. Still, the retelling took well over an hour.

When Mason stopped talking, Nicholson clapped his hands together, jumped to his feet, and paced the floor. He stopped and looked down at Mason, still seated. "You're absolutely sure the man you killed was Edward Low?"

"I am. I was on his ship for over two weeks. His crew usually referred to him as Ned. He had a close relationship with Charles Harris, whom, as I said, lost the battle with a royal frigate. You can be quite assured, Edward 'Ned' Low is dead."

"That is simply wonderful news, Mister Mason. This colony, in fact, all the colonies, will forever be in your debt."

Mason simply nodded as he got to his feet. "It truly was my pleasure to have been of service."

"We may call on you again, Mister Mason. You seem to be a man of some ability."

Without comment, Mason smiled.

The other men got to their feet.

"I'm sure we've taken up enough of the governor's time," Loughton said. He turned to Nicholson. "If there's nothing else, we'll be on our way."

"No, nothing more," Nicholson said with a broad smile. He gave Mason a subtle nod and bid everyone farewell.

On the street, Mason and the others thanked Loughton for his help, his hospitality, and then headed toward Bay Street and the wharves.

Just over two hours later, with the sun directly overhead, they were home.

Charlie and Forrest secured the sloop to the dock and then followed Mason and Jeremy toward the house.

Karen, Lisa, and little Michael vaulted from the back door and raced across the yard into waiting arms.

"I thought for sure you were dead," Karen said to Mason, as she wrapped both arms around his waist and planted her head against his chest.

"Took a little longer than I expected," Mason said.

"You think?" Karen replied. "No word for weeks. We were beyond worry."

"I'm sorry about that," Mason said. "There wasn't much I could do about it after I went aboard Low's ship."

Karen stepped back and peered into Mason's eyes. "Low, what became of him?"

"He's dead," Mason said. "And at the end, he knew exactly why."

Karen and Lisa each hugged Charlie and Forrest before the gaggle began walking toward the house.

Mason walked with his arm wrapped around Karen's waist. "Anything exciting happen around here?"

"Mister Edwards from the trading tavern is dead," Lisa said.

"I heard," Mason said, as he focused on Mato, approaching from the work barn. "Loughton seemed to suspect Mato." He faced Karen. "Did something happen?"

"It did," Karen said. "It could have been a lot worse. Once you're bathed and dressed in fresh clothes, I'll fill you in on the details."

"So, Mato was involved, then?"

"I owe Mato my life. And that's all I'll say on the matter until after you've had a bath." She looked around at the others. "That goes for all you men."

Mason stopped and stared at her as she continued walking.

◆◆◆

After dinner in the common dining room, everyone moved to the back porch for a glass of port. It had become somewhat of a habit over the prior few months, to sip some port and talk after dinner as the sun set.

Mason filled everyone's glass and then took a seat next to Karen. "Did I mentioned Forrest will be staying with us for the foreseeable future, for as long as he wants?"

"You didn't," Karen said, as she and Lisa turned their heads toward Forrest. "But he is most welcome."

"Decided I needed to do something besides run a tavern in New York. Never cared much for that city, now, or in the future."

Charlie cocked his head as he poured another glass of port.

"Figure of speech," Forrest said. "I managed to accumulate a few coins. The place was never really mine to begin with, and Tom will be a much better owner. He practically lives there as it is."

"Tom?" Lisa asked.

"One of the patrons," Mason said.

"We have plenty of space," Lisa said. "And we'll have to find you a wife." She picked Michael up from the floor and placed him on her lap.

"So, what are we working on around here?" Forrest asked.

"Growing season is coming up," Mason said. "We'll all be busy with that."

"Especially transporting the rice to La Florida," Jeremy said. "We have two, maybe three more years to make the payments on this place."

"But even when it's paid for, we'll still be running rice to St. Augustine," Mason said. "I have an agreement with the governor, General Antonio Benavides. Plus, their silver spends much better than colonial paper."

"We still have some worker cottages to build," Jeremy said.

"What about modern conveniences?" Forrest asked.

Lisa shifted Michael to the other leg. "Like what?"

"Indoor plumbing for one, a septic system, the sky's the limit."

"Indoor what?" Charlie asked, as he stared at Forrest.

"Think of it as a privy inside the house," Forrest said.

A shocked expression appeared on Charlie's face. "A privy inside the house, why on earth would you want that? It would stink up the whole place."

Mason cleared his throat. "Jeremy and I, the four of us, really, have discussed such things. But I think it's important we don't get too far ahead of ourselves. We can make small improvements, as we've already done." He motioned toward the bathhouse. "We'll do what we can, but I'm not interested in changing history."

"Exactly," Charlie said, "we don't want to change history." He paused to think about what he had just said, shook his head, and then tipped his glass up and let the wine flow past his lips.

"But we know what's coming."

Mason glanced at Charlie, in the process of refilling his glass.

"We do, and we'll take precautions as much as possible, but anything more would be risky," Mason said.

Karen smiled. "Besides, we have a nice life here and we're in the process of making it better for everyone."

"You mean the slaves?" Forrest said.

"The workers," Lisa corrected.

"That's another example of not getting ahead of ourselves," Mason said. "The time isn't right. To do more than we are would bring risk to us all."

"You're an odd lot," Charlie said with slightly slurred speech.

Mason smiled. "That we are, my friend. And we're happy to call you one of us."

Charlie held his glass up. "I'll drink to that."

Everyone raised their glass and toasted. "To the future," Jeremy said.

CHAPTER 24

The gallows stood ominous between the high and low water marks at Gravelly Point, a spit of land extending into the Newport harbor, Rhode Island Colony. It was a simple affair, given the temporary nature of the occasion, built of three beams erected over a wood platform. A rope with a noose hung from the horizontal beam. Affixed to one corner of the gallows hung the black roger taken from Charles Harris' ship, the Ranger. The folds hid most of the image depicted on the flag, a full-length white skeleton with an hour glass in one hand and a spear in the other, pointed at a red heart. There had been several versions of the flag under which Edward Low, Charles Harris, and Francis Spriggs had sailed. This was an earlier version.

The spot on the sand was without easy access, but that didn't dissuade nearly every citizen of Newport, and those from miles around, from gathering. Some stood on the sand surrounding the gallows. Some occupied small boats held stationary just off shore. This was, after all, a momentous occasion. Never before had so many men been hanged at a single event.

Drinking started early among the town's people. By the time the procession started from the prison on

Bull Street, many of the town's citizens could barely stand. Children and dogs ran through the streets in the festival-like atmosphere. A single drummer, marking each step with a funeral cadence, led the procession, followed by the few remaining citizens and the town sheriff on horseback. He carried a miniature silver oar, a symbol of the admiralty. Behind him, militiamen with muskets herded the condemned.

In all, thirty-eight men had been taken into custody from the ship Ranger. One man died while in jail. The remaining thirty-seven had been tried over a three-day period by the Admiralty Court. They stood accused of piracy before the Honorable William Dummer, Esq., Lieutenant-Governor and commander-in-chief of His Majesty's Province of Massachusetts Bay, New England, along with Samuel Cranston, governor of Rhode Island, and several other duly sworn judges. Of those tried, twenty-six were found guilty and sentenced to be hanged by the neck until dead.

With the procession at its end, those twenty-six men stood in a group, hands tied behind their backs and guarded by the militia.

Among the gathered stood those who had provided testimony during trial. John Welland, captain of the Amsterdam Merchant, was there with a large bandage tied against the right side of his head. It covered the wound left by a missing ear. Captain Peter Solgard and his lieutenant, Edward Smith, were there.

They had described the battle with Low and Harris in much detail during the trial. The judges were all there. Every person of any importance from that part of New England was there.

Most of the citizens stood in solemn silence, each aware that never before had so many men been hanged at one time in Rhode Island, perhaps all of the colonies. It would be the event of the decade, much talked and written about.

James Franklin, older brother to Ben Franklin, was there to observe. He had already published a story in his New England Courant of Boston, detailing Captain Solgard's sea battle with the two pirate ships. He would follow up with a description of the trial and the hangings.

After much milling around and jockeying for a better view amongst the crowd, John Valentine, the Advocate General and the trial's prosecutor, stepped in front of the gallows. He cleared his voice and waited for the murmuring voices to quiet. He turned and faced the twenty-six pirates grouped behind the wood-beamed frame.

Charles Harris stood at the front of the group. He held his chin up. His jaw muscles flexed and his dark eyes bore into the advocate general.

Nearly every other of the convicted stood with his head down, peering at the damp sand at his feet.

Several of the younger men openly wept; their faces gleamed with tears.

A voice among the group suddenly called out. "I was forced to join up. I never signed no articles and never took no money offered."

Valentine waited for the man to finish before he spoke. "His Majesty's court has found you men guilty of piracy on the high seas. You each stand convicted of crimes against man and nature. In May, year of our Lord 1723, you seized the vessel Amsterdam Merchant on the high seas off the coast of New England and carried away beef, gold, and silver, along with a negro slave named Dick. You killed several members of the crew, and you cut off the ear of the vessel's master. These allegations have been testified to and proven beyond doubt. We are gathered here today, in the presence of our Lord, to carry out punishment. Before sentence is carried out, each man will be given a chance to repent before the town's minister."

The man standing to Harris' immediate right, one Daniel Hyde, began whimpering. His body shook and a wet spot began to form at the crotch of his breeches. Within moments, the wet spot extended down both legs. A stream finally broke free, ran down his left shin, and soaked his shoe.

Harris took a side step to the left.

A militiaman, already on the platform, stepped forward and jerked on the rope with one arm to test its strength. Such wasn't necessary since it was a new rope of substantial girth, acquired that morning from the town's general store.

"Let's get on with it," Governor Cranston said, "before we're all swamped with the rising tide."

The Massachusetts Lieutenant-Governor nodded in agreement.

"Bring the first man forward," Valentine said.

Two militiamen grabbed hold of Harris' arms.

"No, not him. Save that man for last. He should witness the demise of his crew."

The militiamen took hold of the still whimpering man to the right and forced him to step up on the platform.

The man began sobbing. His legs buckled.

The militiamen lifted him by the elbows and carried him to the edge of the platform and the waiting hangman.

The hangman, dressed in black breeches, a white linen shirt, a black coat, and topped with a black felt hat, draped the noose over the man's head and tightened the knot around his neck. "Do you want to stand on your own two feet?" the hangman asked. "Or have us toss you out?"

The man got his sobbing under partial control as he extended his legs until his feet touched the wood planks.

The minister, standing next to the hangman, leaned in and whispered a few words in the man's ear.

"Daniel Hyde," Valentine announced, "the court has found you guilty as charged." He nodded to the hangman. "Carry out the sentence."

Without hesitation, the hangman gave Hyde a shove to the center of his back.

Hyde wobbled a bit, finally lost his balance, and fell forward. The toes of his shoes clung to the very edge of the platform while the rest of his body leaned out, suspended by the rope around his neck. He began gagging as he struggled to get a better foothold and pull himself back. His own weight prevented that as he continued to gag.

Members of the assembled crowd oohed and aahed.

The hangman finally kicked the man's feet, sending them flying off the platform. His body swung out, suspended by the rope. The rough texture of the rope chaffed against the man's skin, leaving a bright red line. His neck stretched. His body wriggled and his legs kicked wildly in the air. His eyes bulged as he tried to suck air into his lungs. He gurgled. A foamy stream of saliva ran from the corner of his mouth. After nearly a full three minutes of him twitching, he finally stopped moving.

The hangman reached out and touched the side of his neck. "He's dead."

"Take him down," Valentine said.

Two more militiamen lifted Hyde by his legs, releasing the tension on the rope.

The hangman loosened the knot and slipped the noose from the man's head.

The two militiamen carried the now very much dead Daniel Hyde to a designated spot near the edge of the water and laid him out on the sand.

"Next man," Valentine announced.

One of the convicted men standing in the middle of the group suddenly vomited, sending vestiges of his last meal onto the white shirt of the man standing in front of him.

That man spun around and kicked the man in the groin, sending him to his knees.

"Take one of those men next," Valentine said.

The militiamen did as instructed and selected the man with vomit running down his back. They dragged him through the gaggle and onto the platform, where the minister and the hangman went through the same process.

Mister Franklin recorded the name of each man as they were laid out on the sand, having been hanged.

After an hour and a half, only two of the convicted remained standing: Harris and Joseph Libby.

"Sorry I asked you to join me," Harris said.

"I'm more sorry I agreed," Libby replied. A wide smile of broken and darkened teeth appeared.

"You think Ned got away?"

"Of course he did," Libby said.

"Then we sail with him this day," Harris said, "and forever."

"That we do."

The militiamen took hold of Libby's arms.

Libby shrugged his arms free. "Not necessary gentlemen, I can walk."

"Start walking then," one of the militiamen said.

Libby kept his chin high as he stepped up onto the platform and took the final few steps to the far edge.

The minister leaned in but straightened and took a step back when Libby shook his head.

Without hesitation, the hangman positioned the noose, tightened the knot, and then gave Libby a shove to the back.

Libby didn't fight the inevitable. He took his final step, dropped the four feet, and came to a sudden stop when the rope pulled tight against his skin. His body jerked a few times as involuntary gurgles escaped his lungs. And then he stopped moving. He hung, unmoving except for a slight swing. His eyes remained bulged open.

"Take him down," Valentine said, for all to hear. He turned his attention to the last man standing. "Charles Harris, as master of the vessel Ranger you stand more guilty than all the rest. You led the attack on the Amsterdam Merchant and many other unsuspecting vessels, I'm sure." He paused as he stared at Harris. "Have you anything to say?"

Harris slowly swiveled his head as he scanned the crowd.

Every person in the crowd suddenly stopped talking in anticipation. Hundreds of faces were pointed at Harris.

Harris brought his gaze back to Valentine. "I do not."

At Valentine's beckoning, the militiamen guided Harris onto the platform and out to the edge.

The hangman fastened the noose around his neck.

When the minister leaned in, Harris turned his head away.

The minister stepped back, having not uttered a single word. He turned and left the platform.

Valentine walked from the front of the gallows around to the back, up onto the platform, and out to the edge. He stopped next to Harris. "Charles Harris, you stand convicted of piracy. I shall take great pleasure in seeing you swing." When he got no response from Harris, he took a step back and motioned to the hangman.

The hangman gave Harris a shove.

Harris dropped the four feet, stopped by the jerk of the rope against his neck. His legs kicked a couple of times and his shoulders twitched. Every time he appeared to have stopped moving, and Valentine was about to order him taken down, his body would twitch again. This went on for nearly ten minutes before Harris finally came to rest for the last time.

The militiamen took his body down and carried him to join his twenty-five waiting compatriots, each laid side-by-side in the sand. They laid Harris next to Libby.

As a mass, the crowd shifted from the gallows to the edge of the water, and surrounded the dead bodies.

The air was thick with the smell of body odor, urine, and feces.

A barge was brought around as the crowd looked on in relative silence.

Five men, all volunteers, stepped from the barge and began loading the bodies. With all loaded, they pushed away from the shore and began paddling toward the north end of Goat Island, where the pirates would be buried deep in the sand between the high and low water marks.

With the barge far in the distance, the crowd dispersed, leaving Valentine and James Franklin alone at the water's edge.

"I think your actions here today will forever change the face of piracy along these shores," Franklin said. "It will not be forgotten. Every man and woman in these colonies will hear of it. I'll see to that."

For several moments, Valentine continued to stare at the barge, now a speck in the distance. He finally lifted his chin in acknowledgement, turned, and walked away.

EPILOGUE

September 1760

Dressed in fine petticoats, with her gray hair in a bun, the old woman opened the back door and shuffled onto the porch.

A tall black man in his middle forties, dressed in shoes, breeches, stockings, coat, and hat followed her out. He carried a folded newspaper.

"Husband, you have a visitor," the woman announced.

An old man, with deep wrinkles, white hair, and a beard, leaned forward in his rocking chair. "And who might that be?" he muttered with a weak voice. Even wearing long pants, a long, green coat, and high black boots, it was obvious the man was thin and frail.

"Joe-Turner has come to visit," she said.

"Hello, Mister Mason," Joe-Turner said, as he stepped past the woman and around so the old man could see him without wrenching his neck.

Mason sat back in the chair and smiled. "Joe-Turner, pull up a chair."

The man hesitated. He looked at the nearest chair for several moments before glancing up at the woman still standing in the open doorway.

She motioned her chin toward the empty chair.

Joe-Turner slid into the seat and leaned back as he perused the fields off to the left, and the river directly in front. The scene was brightly lit in the morning sun.

Mason cranked his neck around at the woman. "Maybe some tea for our guest."

"Of course," the woman said, as she closed the door and stepped off the porch toward the outside kitchen.

The two men watched her walk away.

"How is Miss Karen getting on?" Joe-Turner asked.

"Slowing down," Mason said. "We all are."

"And Mister Jeremy? I was real sorry about Miss Lisa."

Mason dropped his chin a few moments. "It was nice of you to come to the funeral." He stared at the river for almost a full minute.

Joe-Turner turned his gaze in that direction, not wanting to press the old man. He waited patiently.

"What was it you asked me?" Mason finally asked.

"Mister Jeremy."

"Oh, he's doing fine. No spring chicken, but he's fine. Been spending most of his time in the work barn. Up early; back late. Don't blame him wanting to stay busy. Wish I could help more."

"Mister Mason, you've done enough for ten men."

At that moment two young children, a boy and a girl, came busting through the back door. "Morning, Grandpa," they both said in unison, as they leapt from the porch and kept running. "Morning, Joe-Turner," they both said over their shoulders.

"And Mister Michael? He doing alright?"

"Fine as a fiddle," Mason said. "Right as rain. He's seeing to the crops."

The back door swung open again and a middle-aged, very pretty woman emerged. She wore a fine set of floor-length petticoats and a thigh-length, brown coat cinched tight at the waist. A tri-cornered hat sat atop her blond, pinned-up hair.

Joe-Turner got to his feet and bowed. "Morning, Miss Emily."

"Morning, Joe-Turner."

"Where you off to this morning?" Mason asked, still seated.

"Going riding with Michael," she smiled. "He'll be waiting for me at the barn."

"You know how impatient he can be," Mason said. "Will you be back for lunch?"

"A short ride, before the heat gets up," she said. "Please keep an eye on little Stephen and Melissa. You know how much trouble they can get into."

"We'll see you for lunch," Mason said.

Emily did a slight curtsy, smiled, and stepped down from the porch. She began walking away.

"It's like Grand Central Station around here," Mason said.

Joe-Turner shook his head. "That's what I remember most about you, Mister Mason. Always saying things people don't understand."

"They will, one day," Mason said.

"So, how are you feeling?"

"A little tired," Mason said. "But all these goings on keeps my mind sharp. That's the most important thing."

"It is, Mister Mason. That it is." He glanced at the newspaper in his hand. "Oh, I brought you a copy of the latest Gazette." He extended his hand toward Mason.

Mason's head wobbled a bit, like he was falling asleep, and his eyes closed.

"Mister Mason, the Gazette, fresh off the press."

Mason opened his eyes, turned his head slightly, and focused on the paper in Joe-Turner's hand. He took the paper and placed it in his lap. "How's the war going?"

"We won a naval battle in the north. Sunk all the French vessels on the Restigouche River. Nova Scotia. But that was months ago. Part of a campaign to isolate the French forts."

"Couple more years and it will all be over," Mason said.

"People say this could go on for many years," Joe-Turner said.

"Nope, couple of years," Mason said.

"Can I quote you on that?" A broad smile spread across Joe-Turner's face.

"Better not," Mason said. "They'll find out soon enough. Anything else?"

"The governor's wife had a baby."

"That's good, babies are always good." Mason's eyes closed again.

Joe-Turner looked up as Karen stepped onto the porch with a cup of tea in each hand.

"Is he sleeping?" Joe-Turner asked, motioned toward Mason. He got to his feet.

"I most certainly am not," Mason said with renewed vigor in his voice. "You were telling me about the war and those dastardly French. They'll be our closest allies one day soon."

"The French?" Joe-Turner asked.

"They'll come to the aid of this nation," Mason said. "They'll take their time about it, but they'll show up when it counts."

Joe-Turner shook his head and looked at Karen, still holding the two cups.

"Stop talking that silliness," Karen said, as she bent at the waist and placed the two cups on a table. She looked at Joe-Turner. "Don't pay him any mind. How's your work?"

"Mister Timothy is keeping me busy with the printing. Business is booming with the war and all."

"He paying you like he said he would?" Mason asked.

"A fair wage, every week," Joe-Turner said. "And me and Sassy still have the small room in the back. We take our meals there, mostly leftovers from what Sassy brings back from the tavern. We're doing just fine."

"You should try writing something," Karen said, as she sat in a chair. "Get Peter's approval before you print anything."

"I already write. The obits mostly."

Karen was about to comment when Mason interrupted.

"How's your lessons?" Mason asked.

"Hush up, you old goat," Karen said. "Joe-Turner finished his lessons years ago. He learned everything me and Lisa had to teach him. He can read and write as well as anyone."

"Mister Timothy seems to like my work. I can thank you kind folks for that. For putting in a word for me."

"There will come a day when the black man won't have to rely on anyone other than himself for his success," Mason said.

Joe-Turner swiveled his head. "What do you mean?"

"No more slavery," Mason said. "About a hundred years."

Joe-Turner scrunched his face. "No more slavery?"

"He just means things are bound to change," Karen said.

"I could tell you things about the future you wouldn't believe," Mason said.

"Please don't," Karen said, matter-of-factly. "Drink your tea before it gets cold."

Mason lifted the cup and saucer from the table and lowered them to his leg.

Karen glanced at Joe-Turner. "Drink your tea," she said, as she turned her head back to Mason. She focused on the newspaper which had fallen to the floor next to Mason's chair. "Is that the South Carolina Gazette?"

"Latest copy," Joe-Turner said. "Mister Timothy wrote an article about the war. French and Indian War they call it."

Karen bent over and retrieved the folded newspaper.

"I was going to read that," Mason said.

She laid the paper on the table. "I'll read it to you, later." She turned to Joe-Turner. "His eyesight isn't what it once was."

"I heard that," Mason said.

"It's the truth," Karen said. "You're getting old, my dear."

"Who are you calling old?"

"Drink your tea," Karen said. She turned her focus to Joe-Turner. "I plum forgot to ask. How's Sassy?"

"The misses is doing just fine. She was in the bed for a week, but she's up and around now." Movement in his periphery caught his attention. He focused on Jeremy, walking toward the house. As he stepped up on the porch, Joe-Turner got to his feet and extended his hand. "Mister Jeremy."

Jeremy shook his hand. "Joe-Turner, what brings you out this way?"

"Wanted to check on you folks and drop off a copy of the latest paper."

"That was very kind of you," Jeremy said, as he took a seat in the chair next to Karen. He leaned in to Karen. "How's he doing?"

"Tired," Karen said. "Not eating much."

"Has Mister Mason been feeling poorly?" Joe-Turner asked.

"He turned eighty-four in August," Jeremy said. "He spends most of his day in that chair, staring at the river."

"Probably thinking about the many adventures you all had," Karen said. "You, Mason, and Forrest. And Charlie."

"I remember Mister Charlie," Joe-Turner said. "He was always nice to me. I remember when Mister Forrest came to stay here. It was sad when they left this world."

"We miss them and think of them every day," Karen said.

A crash gave everyone a start and the three of them turned in unison to Mason.

His head was back against the chair and his eyes were closed. The tea cup and saucer lay in pieces, in a puddle, next to his chair. The tea ran off in rivulets toward the edge of the porch.

Karen jumped to her feet. "Mason!"

"He's just asleep," Jeremy said. "He falls asleep out here every day."

Karen took hold of Mason's wrist. She held it a few moments and then placed two fingers against his neck. After a few more moments, she lowered her knees to the floor, lowered her head to Mason's thigh, and took hold of his hand. A tear escaped from the corner of her eye.

◆◆◆

October, 1760

Vessels of all sizes and shapes lined the shore of the Jackson Plantation and over a hundred people stood at the family cemetery, a manicured plot of land near the work barn. Several granite headstones protruded from the ground. But the people gathered on this sunny afternoon were there to commemorate one in particular.

Per Mason's request years earlier, Karen Mason had asked for a small funeral of close family and friends, and it was, five weeks earlier. But the governor himself persuaded Karen to host a more elaborate ceremony so Mason's many associates could pay their respects. Karen finally relented and the invitations went out. And now, that day had arrived. Karen was most thankful it was not raining.

Every member of the plantation's work force—men, women, and children—stood off to one side, well behind the honored guests. They murmured among themselves and watched the comings and goings of one fine ensemble of clothes after another. Unknown to those guests, every original slave on the Jackson Plantation, all fifty of them, had been freed within five years after Mason and Jeremy acquired the property. And of those fifty, only eight elected to leave the plantation. Each worker was given a formal document attesting to their freedom. And every newborn after that was, by virtue of their free parents, also free. The current work force consisted of many families, some quite large.

Joe-Turner Washington and his wife stood with the other workers. No one referred to him by his last name, most people didn't even know it. It was just Joe-Turner. After Karen and Lisa taught him to read and write, he devoured every written word he could get his hands on. He borrowed all the books the plantation had to offer, and any Mason brought back from his many excursions on the high seas. When the Gazette started up in '32, Joe-Turner found a way to acquire every issue. Much later, when the current owner, Peter Timothy, became post master general and had to divide his time between that and the print shop, Mason persuaded him to take Joe-Turner on as a helper, and as a free man working for a wage. It would have been unheard of in most situations, but Timothy's father, Lewis, had worked for Ben Franklin in Boston before starting his own paper in Charlestown. The father passed on his progressive inclinations to the son, Peter. So, it didn't take that much persuasion to get Joe-Turner a spot in the shop. That had been nearly twenty years earlier.

Mason, Karen, Jeremy, and Lisa had done as much as possible over the years to improve the life of the workers. Any wanting to leave the plantation were given enough spending money to get them where they wanted to go and sustain them for a few months until they could find the kind of life they wanted. Joe-Turner was just one of numerous beneficiaries. But although every worker present on this day was a free man or women, they knew it was something that couldn't be flaunted, especially to those in authority. And there were plenty of those people milling around, waiting for the ceremony to begin.

Acting South Carolina governor William Bull II, dressed in his finest blue long coat and a powdered wig, stood next to Mason's headstone, talking to Karen, Michael, and Emily. He and Mason hadn't been friends exactly, which was true for most of the governors Mason dealt with over the years, but they did exchange a mutual respect for each other. Mason had never turned down a request by any of the South Carolina Colony governors. He answered the call numerous times, nearly dying in the process twice.

In addition, there were people from as far away as Boston and New York; most were businessmen engaged in the trade of commodities. They had all been involved with Mason, in one way or the other, for years.

And it was Mason who had posed the idea of a Charlestown newspaper to Ben Franklin. And when Lewis Timothy wanted to go off on his own, Mister Franklin helped make it happen, to Charlestown's benefit.

Everyone in the crowd suddenly turned to the sight of another vessel arriving, a masted longboat. A small flag, the Cross of Burgandy, a red, saw-toothed cross over a white background, waved from the top of the mast. It signaled the arrival of Lucas Fernando de Palicio y Valenzuela, governor of Spanish Florida. His invitation had gone out, but his attendance had been far from assured. Britain and Spain were not currently at war, but there were rumors Spain would enter the French & Indian War, the Seven Years War in Europe, on the side of France. But even if the two countries had been at war, common decency would have allowed the La Florida governor's attendance. The fact that governor Bull had co-signed the invitation probably went a long way toward Governor Fernando's appearance. It would provide an opportunity for the two men to talk.

The Spanish governor's small party of eight men stepped from the longboat and proceeded in a loose formation toward the large party gathered at the cemetery. All eight men, including the governor leading the way, were dressed in formal military uniforms consisting of long, blue coats over matching breeches and white stockings. Although the governor's uniform included additional and more elaborate ornamentation.

The governor was first welcomed by Jeremy and Karen. They stepped forward and offered their hands.

Jeremy had met with the governor during the last two deliveries of rice to St. Augustine. In recent years, it was just Jeremy who made the trips, since Mason had not been able, due to his health. Mason had never met this particular governor since he had assumed office in 1758, after Mason stopped making the trips. But he was well aware of Mason's initial offer forty years earlier to provide rice to general-governor Antonio Benavides Bazán y Molina and the yearly trips thereafter.

"Governor, may I present Karen Mason."

Governor Fernando dipped his head and kissed the back of Karen's hand. "Very honored to make your acquaintance, madam. Senior Jackson has mentioned you."

"I'm very happy you could make the trip, Governor Fernando." She performed a slight curtsy. Please, let me introduce you to some of our friends."

The last guest to arrive was an aging and frail Indian, accompanied by two braves. His canoe at the water's edge went unnoticed. It wasn't until Karen looked up and saw him ambling toward the cemetery that his presence became known. She tapped Jeremy on the shoulder and pointed. The two of them walked to meet their oldest friend.

Mato wore buckskin, head to toe. The bottom half of his face in earlier years would have been painted black but he had since dispensed with the paint. But he did wear the semi-circle of black and gray feathers, arranged at a slight angle, on top of his head. He also wore a thin, metal bracelet on his left wrist, the same missing-in-action bracelet Mason had given him the very first day they met. And despite his age, and a limp, he stood tall and straight.

Jeremy stepped ahead of Karen and met the Indian. "I didn't think you would make it."

"I not miss honor given my friend," Mato said with a very weak voice.

Jeremy glanced back at Karen.

She stood ten feet back, staring at Mato. Tears ran down her cheeks as she tried desperately to control her emotions.

Mato shuffled forward until he stood directly in front of Karen. He laid the palms of both hands on her two shoulders.

Jeremy, in all his years, had never seen an Indian cry, especially Mato. But he was seeing it now. Mato's expression remained stoic, as always, but his eyes gleamed with moisture.

Karen took a step forward and wrapped both arms around his waist. She held that position for several moments before finally stepping back. She wiped her cheeks with the backs of both hands and then took hold of Mato's elbow. "Come, there are people I want you to meet."

Over the next hour, people mingled and talked. Mostly, they told stories about Mason. Some talked about the first time they met; several talked about the time Mason saved their lives.

When Karen figured everyone had been standing long enough, she motioned to Jeremy.

Jeremy walked the few paces, stood behind Mason's headstone, and cleared his voice.

Off to the side, propped up in a straight-back chair for all to see, was a painting that depicted much younger versions of Mason, Karen, Jeremy, Lisa, and a ten-year-old Michael. It was the only painting in existence that included Mason. He had insisted on a painting of the family at that time, and had searched far and wide for a suitable artist. It had been on display in the main room of the house ever since it was completed. Mason had made sure everyone knew, no matter what happened to the house, the painting must be preserved. That edict had been drilled into every member of the family, starting with Michael, as soon as he was old enough to understand.

Many of the guests had perused the painting; several had studied it for some time. And nearly every one of them asked about the gold object in Mason's right hand. Of course, Jeremy and Karen couldn't tell them the truth, that it was Mason's gold badge from when he was a Federal Air Marshal. Details of the object were obscured enough to claim ignorance, which they did.

"Ladies and gentlemen, may I have your attention."

The conversations lingered a few moments but then, finally, everyone turned to face Jeremy.

Karen, Michael, and Emily moved to his side.

"First of all, the family would like to thank everyone for coming. We very much enjoy being surrounded on this day by people who knew Mason." He scanned the crowd for a moment and then continued, "I arrived in this area on a sunny day, much like today, almost exactly forty years ago. It wasn't by design; it was purely accidental. I didn't know it then, but it was the most fortuitous event of my life. That was the day I met Stephen Mason." He turned his head to Karen. "And his future wife, Karen Mason. I believe it was Karen James back then."

Karen smiled and nodded.

Jeremy turned back to the crowd. "As it turned out, that's the day I also met my future wife." He turned his head and stared at another headstone, a few feet away. "She's resting right over there." He raised his head after several moments. "We arrived here with others who are also no longer with us. Too soon, they departed this world at the hands of a pirate. And while there was nothing Mason could have done to prevent it, he made sure their deaths didn't go unanswered. In very short order, it was just the four of us—Mason, Karen, Lisa, and me. We were alone in an unfamiliar country. But we weren't alone. We met people along the way who would become lifelong friends. The first was a Catawba brave. He's with us today and he stands right over there." He pointed at Mato. "Had it not been for him, we would not have survived those early days." He paused for several moments as he scanned the faces in the crowd. "But we're here to celebrate the life of

Stephen Mason. It was his idea to acquire this property and work the land. He made it happen, with the help from many who became very close to us." He glanced at Joe-Turner and the other workers standing behind him.

"Mason was a rare individual. If he said he would do something, he did it, he kept his word. He valued friendships, loved his family. He came to love this place and this time. He will never be forgotten." Jeremy glanced at Karen and then back to the crowd. "We've set up tables at the house. Please join us for something to eat and drink while we remember Stephen Mason." He pointed. "Michael and Emily will lead the way."

As the crowd began moving off toward the house, Karen joined Jeremy at Mason's headstone. They walked around to the front and stared down at the engraving.

"He will appreciate that," Karen said.

"He will," Jeremy agreed. He stared at the headstone a few more seconds before turning to the family painting, which he plucked from the chair. "Let's get this back inside the house and out of the sun."

◆◆◆

The Present

Matilda Mason walked side-by-side with an older, heavy-set man across the yard. She was on the portly side herself, also middle-aged. Her auburn hair was cut short, just off her shoulders, and she wore a long, flower-print dress.

The man to her side wore slacks and a long-sleeve, button-down shirt.

They chatted about the weather and the latest happenings in Charleston as they walked. They had covered over two hundred yards, from the main house to the far edge of the property, when they came to the family cemetery and an equally middle-aged man on his knees pulling weeds from around a headstone.

"He insists on doing that himself," Matilda said. "Won't let anyone else tend to the graves." She and the man to her side stopped a few feet from the man at work. "Michael, we have a guest."

Michael Mason looked around, got to his feet, and stared at the man to his wife's side. "The policeman who visited us a few months ago." He glanced at Matilda. "You were shopping that day." He turned back to the man. "I've forgotten your name."

"Mike Reeves. I came here before, asking about a missing associate."

"Yes, of course, did you ever find your friend?"

"I did," Reeves said. He glanced at the headstone at Michael's feet.

"Did you offer Mister Reeves something to drink?" he asked Matilda.

"She did, but I only wanted to stop by briefly."

"What can I do for you?" Michael asked, as he stepped forward and shook Reeves' hand. "More questions about that missing person?"

"No, I just wanted to stop by on my way through."

Michael cocked his head.

"I retired from the Federal Air Marshall's Service. Bought a place in the mountains, near Ashville. This was on the way and thought I would stop by."

"Glad you did," Michael said. "You caught me in the middle of some yard work, but we can head back up to the house."

"You keep it up yourself?"

"I do. I guess I feel obligated to carry on the tradition. No, not obligated; privileged. It started with one of the early ones." He pointed to a headstone.

Reeves stepped closer. "Hard to read, must have been here quite a while."

Michael stepped to his side. "Karen Mason. That was the original Mason's wife. Stephen Mason. She began looking after the plots after Stephen died. For each subsequent generation, the task fell to the oldest. These days, that would be me."

Reeves looked around the cemetery at the numerous headstones. He spotted two together, off to the side, and walked over. "Jeremy Jackson." He looked to the next. "And Lisa."

"Those were the original owners," Matilda said. "The property passed into the Mason line when Jeremy died."

"You mentioned that the last time I was here, but seeing them, it makes it all real." His head was on a swivel as he walked among the markers. "You have some non-Masons here." His eyes focused on two stones. "Charlie Sievert, Forrest J. Gerber," he read.

"Had to be close friends," Matilda said. "There were more markers on a former part of the property, sold eighty or so years ago. Nearly half a mile from here. The current owner found the stones not long ago. Probably the slave cemetery."

Michael bent down to pull a weed. "Mostly Masons here, though. There were a lot of them through the years."

Reeves looked around again and then walked back to the headstone Michael had been working on. "Hard to read," he said, as he knelt down. "This is Mason's final resting spot? I'm sorry, Stephen."

Michael nodded. "Next one over is Karen. The engraving is almost unreadable."

Reeves ran his index finger over the slight indentions. "Stephen Mason." He looked closer at the engraving just below. "There's no year of birth, just a dash and 1760, the year he died, I presume."

"That's true of the original four," Matilda said. "Stephen Mason, Karen, and the Jacksons. Just a dash with no year of birth."

Reeves twisted his torso to look up at Michael and Matilda. "Any reason ever given?"

"No," Michael said, "none at all. We just figured no one knew their year of birth. I do know Stephen was in his eighties when he died."

Reeves turned back to the stone and stared at the engraving just below the date. He leaned closer to read the inscription. "Devoted husband, father, and friend, unbounded by space and time, now free to return home." Reeves got to his feet. "Seems most appropriate."

"Sure we can't interest you in a glass of tea back at the house?" Michael asked.

"Actually, you can," Reeves said, as he continued to stare at Mason's headstone. "It took some time, but you made it back my friend," he murmured.

"What was that?" Michael asked.

"Nothing." He looked up with a smile. "A glass of tea would be nice."

As the three of them walked toward the house they chatted about the property and the people in the cemetery.

As Michael stepped up on the porch, he stopped and turned back to Reeves. "I don't believe you ever mentioned the name of the fellow you were looking for."

"You're right, I never did."

Matilda stepped up on the porch next to her husband and looked down at Reeves. "What was his name?"

Reeves just stared at them for several moments. He finally twisted his torso as he surveyed the land leading back down to the cemetery. He turned back and looked up at the two faces still waiting for an answer. "His name." He took in a deep breath and exhaled. "His name was Stephen Mason."

A REQUEST FROM THE AUTHOR

Thank you for reading *The Punishers*. I hope you enjoyed the story as much as I enjoyed writing it. I do have one request. I ask that you please take a few moments to enter a product review on your Amazon Orders page. Independent authors depend on reviews to get their books noticed. And reviews also help make my future books better. A few moments of your time would be much appreciated. I look forward to reading your thoughts. —**Victor Zugg**

ABOUT THE AUTHOR

Victor Zugg is a former US Air Force officer and OSI special agent who served and lived all over the world. Given his extensive travels and opportunities to settle anywhere, it is ironic that he now resides in Florida, only a few miles from his hometown of Orlando. He credits the warm temperatures for that decision.

Check out the author's other novels—*Solar Plexus (1)*, *Near Total Eclipse (Solar Plexus 2)*, *Surrounded By The Blue*, *From Near Extinction*, and, of course, *A Ripple In Time*, books 1 and 2.

Printed in Great Britain
by Amazon